Mistletoe, Moonlig[ht]
A Ravenwood Cove M[ystery]
By Carolyn L. Dean

Want to know about new releases, sale pricing, and exclusive content? My email newsletter is HERE. Spam-free, and only sent out when there's something new, on sale, or FREE. I PROMISE.

MISTLETOE, MOONLIGHT, and MURDER is copyright 2016 by Carolyn L. Dean. All rights reserved. This book or any portion thereof may not be reproduced or used in any manner whatsoever without the express written permission of the author or publisher, except for the use of brief quotations in critical articles or reviews.

1

DEDICATION

For those who believed in me and those who did not. You *both* have motivated me to write.

For the amazing community of cozy mystery readers. I'm having such a good time getting to know you, and reading the books you recommend!

For **Jon,** who's both an excellent brother and a great expert to consult.

Table of Contents

Chapter 1 4
Chapter 2 12
Chapter 3 20
Chapter 4 25
Chapter 5 33
Chapter 6 38
Chapter 7 43
Chapter 8 50
Chapter 9 59
Chapter 10 72
Chapter 11 75
Chapter 12 85
Chapter 13 92
Chapter 14 97
Chapter 15 100
Chapter 16 107
Chapter 17 111
Chapter 18 116
Chapter 19 120
Chapter 20 128
Chapter 21 135
Chapter 22 140
Chapter 23 144
Chapter 24 152

Chapter 25 156
Chapter 26 165
Epilogue 171
AUTHOR NOTES: 176
RUTH'S CASHEW CHRISTMAS COOKIES
.... 178

Chapter 1

"It looks like Christmas exploded all over the inside of your coffeeshop."

Meg pushed a stray blonde curl behind one ear and surveyed her handiwork critically. It had taken her most of the morning to decorate Cuppa with huge silver garlands and hanging red glass balls, not to mention the dozen or so strings of colored lights she'd carefully stapled to the ceiling and walls. She frowned a bit at Amanda's blunt critique.

"Hey, I love Christmas, and we've got to do something to compete a bit more with Ivy's Café. Did you know they're starting to put out board games and free newspapers on the tables after the breakfast rush?" She brushed her hands together, apparently temporarily done with her decorating, and folded the metal stepstool shut. "Nobody can say we don't have the Christmas spirit, and if it brings in more customers that's definitely an added bonus."

Amanda took a sip of her mocha and settled back into the overstuffed chair in contentment. Meg had added a subtle dash of cinnamon to the top, and it seemed to match the holiday mood perfectly. The only other customer, a bundled-up tourist with a metal detector leaning against his small table, seemed completely engrossed in his smartphone. Amanda wasn't surprised when her bubbly friend plopped down in the chair next to her, a huge grin on her face. No customers to wait on meant more time to chat.

"You'll never guess what my grandmother told me." Meg's face was expectant.

"I'm scared to ask."

Amanda knew better than to venture a guess. Meg's ninety-year-old grandmother, Mrs. Granger, may have looked like just an old lady with a walker, but she knew more about what was going on in Ravenwood Cove than a detective, a bloodhound, and a fortuneteller combined. She spent a lot of time quietly eavesdropping while she sat and knit on a bench by the warm woodstove in Petrie's hardware store, chatting with everyone and learning about the lives of most of the small beach town's residents.

Meg leaned forward, her eyes showing her excitement.

"You know that big empty shop next to Truman's bike and kite store? The one that's been vacant forever?"

Amanda knew it. It was rumored that the owner was some investor in Eugene that had bought it as a tax write-off, and then hadn't bothered to even remove the plywood sheets nailed over the big front windows. The shop shared a common wall with Truman's bike and kite shop, Ride the Wind, and the local florist was on the other side, with only a narrow alley in between them. Years before, the old place had been a store for auto parts, but it had been closed up for ages, and the townspeople had been grumbling about its sorry state ever since.

"Truman bought it." Meg's voice had an edge of glee in it, and Amanda's eyebrows went up in surprise.

"He bought it? I didn't think Truman had that sort of cash."

Meg shrugged and continued, wanting to get her whole story out. "I guess he does. Anyway, Gram told me that he's decided his kite and bike store won't be a good business over the winter months because of the Oregon weather, so he's going to expand and open a bookstore, too." Meg was practically bouncing up and down in her seat and Amanda grinned, knowing how much her friend loved to read. "It's going to have used books as well as new ones, and some comfy chairs for people who want to stay and read a bit. Gram says he's going to call it Benny's Books."

It made perfect sense that Truman would name his new store that. His little brown dog, Benny, was his constant companion wherever he went. Benny was a half-dachshund, half-Chihuahua mutt, and all friendly all the time. More than one person had secretly set aside a stash of dog biscuits in case Benny happened to stop by. Even though his owner Truman had only moved to town a few months before, he'd made quite an impression on the residents of Ravenwood Cove. Maybe his tattoos and constantly changing wild haircuts had put some people off at first, but his huge grin and willingness to help others quickly made him friends, including Amanda. The first time she'd seen a trio of cotton-haired church ladies clustered around Truman at a potluck, soberly discussing casserole recipes with him in rapt fascination, she knew he was going to be just fine, even if his hair did sometimes have orange or purple tips.

"Wow! That *is* big news! When's he going to open it?"

"I guess the paperwork's already done, and the first shipments of books are on their way. Gram says he's going to try to catch the Christmas shoppers, so he may be open this week, even if everything isn't quite ready yet. He's got the bookshelves made and everything."

Amanda set her coffee cup down and sighed. "I can't believe I didn't know about this. I've been so buried with work at the Inn that I haven't talked to people much lately, I guess."

"Well, with the farmers market closed down for the winter you haven't needed to talk with the merchants as much and besides, you've been busy. Except for those cottage rentals down by the cannery, the Ravenwood Inn is the only real place for tourists to stay when they're in town." Meg reached down next to her chair and dug around in a paper bag, finally pulling out two more thick strands of tinsel garland, this time in green. "You and Jennifer have been so busy making sure that people are happy at the Inn that you haven't taken much time for yourselves." She shook an accusatory finger at Amanda. "Even if you are still doing renovation on the Inn – "

"Just the parts the guests aren't staying in," Amanda interjected, feeling a bit defensive.

Meg nodded, showing she understood. "Okay, so you're not restoring the floors and painting the walls in front of the guests. You still need some time off. I know you've been doing a lot of work on the canned food drive for the food bank. I never see you stop working, and Jennifer seems to be at the Inn all the time, too."

"Someone needed to organize the food drive," Amanda said firmly. "And running an inn is hard work sometimes."

The truth was, Amanda wouldn't want any other job in the world. She loved her historic inn, even if she was still renovating it to its former glory. That reminded her, she needed to call the gutter cleaning guy to get the dead leaves out, and buy some smoked salmon for the incoming guests. She also needed to rake the old foliage out of the front flower beds and look into a linen delivery service and...

"Just remember that you need some fun, too, okay? I know Roy's going to be taking a month-long vacation over Christmas. Maybe you should check with Solomon and see if he can help you with the remodeling stuff for a bit while Roy's out of town."

Amanda shook her head, adamant. "You know how hard it is to get a good contractor who shows up on time and knows what he's doing? I'll wait for Roy to come back. Besides," she added, "I hear Solomon's more of a small project handyman." She'd seen Solomon around town with his small, battered pickup, and although she'd never heard anything bad about him, she was much more comfortable working with someone she knew.

Meg looped the tinsel garland around her hands, obviously getting ready for another round of over-the-top decorating. "They're going be showing *It's a*

Wonderful Life at the Liberty this week. Why don't you bring James and we'll double?"

"Who are you going to bring as your date?" Amanda had a good idea of what the response would be, and she wasn't disappointed.

"I'll find someone."

Amanda suppressed a smile. "How's the internet dating going?" She tried to keep her voice light, but sometimes she worried about her bubbly friend and her nearly-constant search for Mr. Right. Meg hadn't been lucky in love, that's true, but Amanda wasn't sure that the way she was going about it was going to have the best chance of permanent happiness.

Meg grimaced a bit and shrugged her shoulders. "About the usual. Gotta kiss a lot of frogs before I can find my prince, I guess."

"Just make sure you don't get any warts." Amanda gave her a playful wink and Amanda laughed and threw the wadded-up ball of tinsel at Amanda.

"Hey, I'll be careful. It's not like all of us just have some handsome detective falling into our laps. Some of us have to go out and work a bit harder at finding love."

"He didn't just fall into my lap. And I wouldn't call it love. We've just started dating, that's all." Amanda looped the garland several times and handed it to Meg. "I'll check with James and see what his schedule is, but you know how that can change."

She took a last sip of her coffee and stood up, gathering her raincoat and shrugging it on. "Think I'll stop by and see what's going on with Truman. Did you want me to take Benny those dog treats you talked about having him sample?"

Meg nodded and walked behind the counter, fishing around for a couple of moments before pulling out a small wax bag. "I'm hoping these will be popular enough we can add them as something new for the pet owners to buy, or to give out to dogs when they come in."

Amanda was surprised. "You're going to let dogs into Cuppa?" That was a first.

Meg gestured at the front window, the glass still being pelted by loud rain. "In this weather? Absolutely. We don't have a covered place for the dogs to get out of the rain, and I don't have any trouble with a well-mannered dog coming in with its owner." She handed the bag to Amanda. "Sometimes I like dogs better than I like people. Don't forget your umbrella."

"Trust me, I won't." Peering out the front window doubtfully, Amanda's view of Ravenwood Cove was smeared and blurred by the fat raindrops running down the glass. The sky was a flat, leaden gray. Since she'd moved up from Southern California she'd never seen so much rain. Several of the townspeople had told her that this year's winter weather was unusually soggy, even for Oregon. Stepping out into the blowing drizzle, she gripped her umbrella tightly and headed off to Truman's bike shop.

Chapter 2

Amanda's windshield wipers could barely keep up with the downpour. *It's almost like the rain's blowing sideways,* she thought ruefully, keeping an eye on the brake lights of the car in front of her. She was already regretting her offer to pick up the carved wooden sign that Roy Greeley had made for Truman's new bookstore. The road that led to the small town of Likely was full of potholes and twists, and in the dim, late afternoon gloom her headlights struggled through the rain to shine any light on the cracked pavement. Even the cheery Christmas music playing on the radio didn't make this trip any more enjoyable.

It had been great to see Truman again and catch up on his big plans for the new bookstore. Like always, he was full of enthusiasm and wild ideas. He'd been happy to point out where the secondhand sofas would be, so that choosy readers could have some time to peruse a book or two before they decided to buy, and to show her where two overstuffed chairs would be placed. Benny had kept pace with his owner, seemingly pleased with the fresh smell of cut wood and maze of tall bookcases. Truman had installed a wide door between his bike and kite shop and the new store, explaining that he'd open it the days he wanted both businesses open, or he could keep it shut and just run one business at a time. When he mentioned possibly hiring someone else to help him out, Amanda made a mental note and started thinking of possible candidates to point in his direction. Winters were tough for some of the residents of Ravenwood Cove, with the lumber industry stalling out and the recent surge of tourists tapering off to a thin, seasonal trickle. Mrs. Granger had mentioned how some families just scraped by, and a new job could be a blessing to many people. Maybe she could point someone his way.

It wasn't too far out of town to get to Roy Greeley's place, just across the road from Sandford Lake. She'd been there a couple of times before, when her contractor had been building special items for the Inn, but the last time she'd showed up to pick up a new porch swing her day had almost ended in disaster. Just as Roy was about to load the swing into the back of Amanda's SUV, they'd heard the high whine of police sirens chasing an armed suspect and had scrambled to take cover in Roy's basement. Waiting and watching from the small window, they'd been safe there, but Amanda hadn't been on the road to Likely since then. Too many disturbing memories.

She was less than a quarter mile from Roy's house when she saw the strangest thing. She'd been concentrating on the road, carefully steering around potholes and following the car in front of her, when a motion on the steep hillside to her right caught her attention.

It was surreal. The trees on the hill were walking down the slope toward the car.

Walking.

She could see them moving, their mostly-bare branches waving as they wobbled a bit, heading straight for the road ahead of her.

Only they weren't actually walking. They were sliding. The entire hillside was sliding, picking up speed

13

as the sodden earth gave way. Tons of rainwater had eroded the soil so deeply that boulders and trees were being pushed along in the churning, inevitable mass, now moving relentlessly downhill.

Amanda frantically hit the horn on her steering wheel, trying to warn the car in front of her, her heartbeat leaping in fear. The dark landslide swept down the slope, accelerating with sudden speed. The lead car must've finally seen the mudslide, but the frantic brake lights of the sedan were too late. The roiling mud slammed into the side of the car, skidding it sideways and off the road. With horrible force, it pushed the small car over the embankment, the brake lights still desperately blinking as the driver tried futilely to keep from going over the edge.

Amanda gasped and slammed her car into reverse. She hit the gas as hard as she could, grateful no one was behind her as she rocketed backward, trying to keep from being engulfed by the tons of earth pouring down the hillside. By the time she was far enough away to jump on her brakes and put her car in park, the landslide had mostly stopped. Small rocks were bouncing down the hill, but the bulk of the huge, muddy mass was settling into heavy stillness. Peering at the deadly mass, she could barely breathe in fear.

She jerked her door open and ran as fast as she could toward where she'd seen the sedan disappear. Wiping the pelting rain from her eyes as she ran, she could just see the right doors of the car, the rest completely encased in unstable mud. Breathing a silent prayer, she eased her way down the slope toward the car, grabbing at small shrubs and tall grass as she did her best to keep from falling down the incline. She tried to keep watch for movement or bouncing rocks as she peered in the passenger side window but the pouring rain and dimming light made it difficult.

The passenger, a man, had his face turned away from her and was loudly groaning. She could see that part of the roof near the man's head had caved in a bit and there was a flat, tinny taste of fear in her mouth as she realized that they probably only had seconds before the landslide moved again and crushed the entire car.

Desperately, she grabbed the door handle and tried to wrest the door open, frantically pulling while trying to keep her feet under her on the slippery grass.

"HEY! Kick out the glass! Can you open the door from your side?" she frantically shouted, nearly dislocating her wrist as she struggled with the stuck door.

The driver seemed to hear the shouting, and rolled his head toward her. Amanda gasped. It was James' brother, Ethan Landon. His eyes didn't look focused, and a cut on his head was streaming bright red blood down the side of his face.

"Ethan! Open the door!"

He blinked his eyes, running a hand across them to try to clear the blood from his right eye. Amanda could tell he was still dazed from the impact.

"Ethan! Kick out the glass!" Her words seemed to be having some impact on him, and he unbuckled his seatbelt. Amanda could hear the metal in the car groan as the weight of the sodden earth and rocks continued to compress it. There was no time to waste. If she didn't get him out, Ethan was going to be crushed to death, and the wall of mud would sweep farther down the slope, taking her with it. She briefly wondered what it would be like to die by landslide.

"ETHAN! I SAID MOVE, MISTER!" she shouted in her best drill sergeant voice, still yanking on the door handle futilely. The passenger side window, flexed by the extreme weight on the car roof, finally shattered like an exploding bomb, spraying brilliant shards of safety glass outward as it broke. The sound seemed to awaken Ethan, and he moved to the window and put his head and shoulders outside, trying to lean forward and push with his elbows enough to escape. Amanda frantically grabbed him under the armpits and pulled with every bit of strength she had, desperately hoping that she'd be able to move a full-sized man in time. Ethan pushed with his feet and he finally slid completely out of the car window, Amanda still grabbing onto him as he rolled to the ground.

"This way!" she ordered, trying to steer him toward the road. The dazed man scrambled along with her as she pulled him away from the landslide and up the sodden embankment, slipping repeatedly as they moved as quickly as possible. They could hear the metal creaking as Ethan's car was slowly pushed and crushed by the landslide, the mud still shifting as tons of dirt and rock above it pressed downward. With a final, last-ditch heave Amanda and Ethan pulled themselves onto the edge of the road, the solid pavement an incredibly welcome sensation.

The climb had been strenuous, and Amanda felt herself gasping for air as she pulled herself to her feet. She could see that Ethan's scalp wound was still bleeding copiously, the scarlet blood being washed down his body by the driving rain. She kept a firm grip on his upper arm as she pulled him toward her car. The headlights were still on, the radio cheerfully singing Christmas carols, the driver side door still open from when she'd sprinted toward the sedan. She opened the passenger door and gently eased Ethan into the seat. Digging around behind him, she grabbed a clean sweatshirt she had stowed in the back seat and showed him where to press it against his head wound. Shutting his door, she raced around to her side of the car, plopping into the seat, her fingers scrabbling around inside her purse. Her heart was racing as she dug out her cell phone. She clicked off the radio.

"Who are you calling?" Ethan was leaning back in the seat and peering at her with one eye, the other covered by the gore-soaked fabric he had pressed to his head.

"Nine one one. I seem to call them a lot. You'd think they'd know my voice by now," she babbled, desperately hoping that she'd get cell reception.

Two bars. That would be enough.

As she punched in the first number she looked up through the foggy windshield. The headlights were shining on something at the base of the landslide. It was striped. Definitely not a rock or tree. She squinted and leaned forward, swiping a hand over the damp glass, trying to figure out what it was.

It couldn't be.

She must be seeing that wrong.

Her heart caught in her throat.

"Wait here."

She got out of the car, not feeling the cold rain pelting her as she slowly walked down the road toward the white object.

It wasn't one object. It was two.

Two feet, one with a dark tennis shoe and one only encased in a striped yellow and green sock.

Someone was lying on their back on the asphalt, covered by tons of mud, only their feet sticking out of the rubble piled on top of them.

Amanda took a deep breath and knelt just far enough away that she could touch the feet. Trying not to gag, she slowly pulled one sock down a bit. As soon as she'd moved it just a couple of inches she could immediately tell that she didn't need to check for a pulse. The dark lines of a bird tattoo just above his ankle were mottled and smeared, in the way only decay could make them.

Whoever this person was, they hadn't been alive for quite some time. No one living would look like that.

Even though she'd only touched the sock, she carefully wiped her fingertips off on her sopping-wet jeans, trying to suppress a shiver. Stumbling quickly back to the car, Amanda squinted against the glare from her car's headlights. The body that was under that landslide was beyond help, but Ethan needed an ambulance and he needed one fast. Sliding gratefully into her seat again, she pulled out her phone.

"Nine one one. What's your emergency?"

"Dead body who won't need an ambulance, and a hurt man who will. Please hurry!"

Chapter 3

"You're in shock."

Amanda looked up at the young paramedic. She was trying to make sense of his words but even though she knew she'd seen him before, she was having trouble focusing enough to remember where they'd met. She vaguely recalled talking to him at the Harvest Festival, and that he had a dog named Rosebud, but she couldn't quite remember the man's name. Leaning back in the reclined front seat of Grace TwoHorses' car, she was grateful that the owner of her favorite toy store, Kazoodles, had been the next person to drive down the road to Likely. Grace was hovering behind the paramedic's shoulder, obviously concerned, as the young man checked Amanda for injuries.

"Your name's Leo Carpinski." It had taken her a bit, but she remembered, and that made her feel a bit better.

"We need to get you warm right away," Leo said, as he listened to her heartbeat with a stethoscope. Amanda gestured wordlessly toward Ethan, who was already in the ambulance with a paramedic attending to him. She could see an IV set up beside him and the paramedic shut the back doors as the ambulance slowly pulled away, finally turning on its lights and siren to get Ethan to the closest hospital.

"He's okay?"

Leo looked her in the eyes, and she had the feeling he was using small, clear words to talk to her.

"He's going to be fine. He's gonna need some x-rays and to get examined, but he'll be okay." He put an oxygen meter on her finger. "Let's worry about you now, all right?"

Grace was still standing nearby, her face showing her worry. "I've got a Pendleton wool blanket in the back of my car. Will that help?"

The paramedic pulled two hot packs out of his medical kit. "I'm going to get some of the wet clothing off her. Let's get these going for some heat, and we'll put the blanket over the top of them. Is that heater turned up all the way?"

Grace quickly checked the car dashboard and nodded. "All the way. It takes a bit to get warm but it should kick in here pretty quick."

As Leo was carefully pulling off Amanda's rain jacket, she looked at her concerned friend, now carrying the wool blanket. "I'm sorry I'm so muddy. I'm getting dirt all over your nice car."

Grace patted her awkwardly. "I'm just glad you're okay, honey. Don't worry about a thing."

It didn't take long for the police to arrive and block off the scene. The huge mudslide had completely covered the road to Likely, but a cordon of yellow crime tape made sure that no one would get too close to the two feet sticking out of the mud. George Ortiz, the police chief, stopped by Grace's car to see how Amanda was doing, but after a quick conversation with the paramedic, held just out of Amanda's earshot, he went straight to work. Several people in town had a hobby of listening to the local emergency channels, using their scanners to find out what was going on in the area, and it was obvious that word had spread quickly. A crowd slowly gathered, keeping a respectful distance from the tape and talking quietly amongst themselves as they speculated who was buried under the tons of wet earth and uprooted trees.

A very familiar unmarked police car pulled up just as the second ambulance arrived, and Amanda sighed. She already knew that James would be concerned, but also knew that he'd probably have something to say about the fact that she was the one who discovered the body.

Again.

Looking at the world sideways because of her reclined seat, she tried to think of what to say as James strode quickly toward her.

"You've got new boots," she commented idly, ignoring the look of concern on his face.

"I'm not going to talk about my boots. Are you okay?"

She opened her mouth to reply but Leo answered for her. "Shock, maybe a sprained wrist, a few small cuts from glass. We're going to take her to the hospital just to make sure, but she should be fine."

James nodded, his face relieved, and the paramedic went to talk to the driver of the second ambulance, which had just arrived.

"Seriously, how are you?"

"Well, I'm covered in stinky mud, and I've touched a dead body." The heat packs and the blanket were doing their work, and she was starting to feel a bit better. "I can tell you that I won't need to use the treadmill today. I've definitely reached my target heart rate." She tried to sit up but he put a gentle hand on her shoulder, obviously wanting her to stay still. Amanda could see the worry in his eyes.

She flashed back to the image of James' brother leaving in the ambulance. "How's Ethan? Did you see him?"

"I called and talked to him. He seemed more concerned that he'd lost his wallet when he escaped the car than about being hurt. Lucky he still had his phone, before the paramedic wrestled it away from him." Amanda smiled at the mental picture of Ethan arguing with the paramedic while the siren was wailing on the ambulance.

James continued. "He told me he's fine, but I've seen him get kicked in the shoulder by a horse and say that." He laid a warm hand on her cheek. "I'll be going to the hospital in a bit, to check on you both." His smile was meant to reassure her, but she could see how stressed he was.

His voice was thick with emotion. "Thank you for saving my brother. George called and told me what you did."

Amanda felt almost embarrassed by his praise, and quickly changed the subject. "Do I get an award for being the first person in Ravenwood Cove to touch more dead guys than the medical examiner?"

"No, but you're getting dangerously close to earning our Frequent Flyer discount. How in the world do you get involved in so much trouble?"

She looked at him ruefully, a thin trickle of muddy water running down her neck. "Just lucky, I guess."

"Well, we don't usually give a trophy for that, and it's not exactly something you can put on your resume."

She bit her lip, thinking over the events of the last hour. "Any idea who that is?"

Her words were vague, but he knew instantly what she meant.

"Not until we dig him out. The crime scene team's on their way." Before she could ask, he answered her question. "Looks like a man's feet, and that's all we know right now."

"Is this normal, finding dead people like this? I mean, how often do people die in this town?"

James smiled and shrugged. "More things happen around here than you probably want to know about. How do you think I keep my job as a detective? I'm not just a pretty face, you know."

Chapter 4

"We don't have any guests arriving until tomorrow morning. I'll bet we can decorate the whole downstairs this afternoon." Meg looked giddy at the prospect, and Amanda could almost see what her bubbly friend must've looked like as an excited little girl.

"Everything but the tree," Amanda commented as she plopped a cardboard box on the sofa. "James says he'll bring me a beauty in a few days, but he won't have time to go up to his folks' ranch and cut one before that."

She brushed her hands together briskly, glad to be done with the dusty boxes they'd dragged down from the Ravenwood Inn's cavernous attic. The old-fashioned Christmas decorations had included everything from metal tinsel to an elaborately-carved wooden nativity scene. The heavy velvet Santa suit, carefully packed in tissue paper and folded in a bag at the bottom of the last box, was an unexpected treasure to find. As soon as Amanda pulled out the luxurious costume she began brainstorming who would make the perfect Santa. There were several men she knew who carried around their own padding and wouldn't need any pillow to have a proper Santa belly.

Amanda had tirelessly questioned Mrs. Granger for every detail she knew about the Ravenwood Inn's past, and her tales of the legendary parties that the Inn used to throw on Christmas Eve were amazing and inspiring. It seemed only fitting that the new owner of the Ravenwood Inn would throw a party for Christmas Eve this year, and being able to continue the tradition of a using the Santa suit just felt right.

Meg was untangling a long string of large lights, a look of concentration on her face. "It's a lot easier to just buy new ones," she finally said in frustration, tossing the jumbled mess into a spare box. "This thing is beyond help."

Amanda smiled at her impatient friend. "We've got time. Here, hand it to me."

Meg watched Amanda carefully untangling the lights. "So, when did you become the Queen of Patience?"

Lights fixed and looped carefully over her arm, Amanda grabbed a small metal hanger. "This is fun, all of it! Even the tedious parts." She pulled the stepladder over to the front window. "You have to understand that when I lived in LA, my boyfriend didn't even like Christmas trees."

Meg looked appalled. "What sort of creep doesn't like Christmas trees? Were you dating Scrooge?"

Climbing up the stepladder, Amanda couldn't help but laugh. "Ken said they were too messy, so we just hung up stockings and went out to eat at a nice restaurant on Christmas Eve. You know how long I've wanted a Christmas tree?" It was nice to finally be able to talk about Ken and not wince at the memory of him. Maybe her new life in Ravenwood Cove was starting to soften some of her bad memories.

Amanda glanced over at the wide area they'd cleared in anticipation of the huge noble fir that was going to go right in front of the main parlor window. She could almost picture it there, lit up and covered with ornaments. In the week since she'd pulled Ethan out of the car, she'd been busy getting ready for the holidays. The front porch of the Inn had already been decorated, with fresh cedar garlands looped between the circular columns holding the porch railing, and wide red ribbons tied in festive bows at every window. A colorful wreath hung on the front door and Amanda had taken the extra effort to hang candle lanterns from the porch ceiling next to the house. With the electric porch light turned off, the gentle glow of the Christmas lights and the flame of the fat pillar candles was beautiful and calm. Amanda had recently started an evening habit of taking a thick quilt and sitting on the padded white wicker sofa out on the porch. The light was too dim to read but she just loved being bundled up out of the weather, listening to the wind in the trees and watching the night sky.

Meg was putting the packing material back in the box. "Where is everybody? I thought Lisa and Jennifer were coming, too."

Amanda gave the hanger a final whack with a hammer and carefully hung the lights inside the window. "I gave Jennifer the rest of the day off. She's got choir practice at the church, and then later she's got another one with the Dickens Carolers." She climbed down the stepladder, slipping the hammer into her belt loop. "Seems like everybody in town's got something to do for the Hometown Holidays coming up. Lisa said she'd be by later."

Jennifer Peetman was both her employee and her friend, and Amanda still blessed the day she'd hired the quiet girl. Always an early bird, she'd already done so much work at the Inn that morning that Amanda was happy to give her some time off. Jennifer was a wonder; always seeming to find something to do to make the guests more comfortable or the Inn run better. It didn't hurt that she just lived next door, and that she was able to whip up a tasty breakfast while keeping a lively conversation going.

There was a knock, the front door opened, and Lisa popped her head around the doorframe.

"Anyone home?" she asked with a grin. "I brought you a visitor." As soon as she came in the room, it was immediately apparent who her guest was. Cupped in her gloved hands was a small gray-striped kitten, looking around curiously.

"Meet Finn," Lisa said happily, setting him down on the patterned carpet. "I left Moski and Jasmine at home." Seeing Amanda's concerned face, she hastily added, "Don't worry, I'll keep an eye on him so he doesn't do something terrible."

"I didn't know the kittens were big enough to be out and about." The last time Amanda had seen them they were still tiny, recently orphaned and curled in a basket under Lisa's newsroom desk. "You'll have to watch for Oscar," she said as she eyeballed the small bundle of fur. "I'm not sure how he's going to take another kitty in his domain. He kind of rules the roost around here."

Meg was already crouched down and cooing over Finn, who closed his eyes in bliss the moment he was scratched under the chin.

"Where did you get the name Moski?"

"It means 'never mind' in the trade language that's used in Papua New Guinea. Since that little guy never minds me when I tell him to stop doing something, it seems only appropriate."

Amanda knew her friend had done quite a bit of exotic travel, but this was new. "You were in Papua New Guinea? How much of the language can you speak?"

"Just enough to tick off anyone who speaks it well," Lisa said with a grin. "I can basically ask how much something costs and then swear at them when they try to overcharge me."

"Ten to one Finn tries to eat the tinsel," Amanda said as she moved the small stepladder out of the way. "Lisa, I thought you were going over to Ethan's place to check on him."

"Already did. I stopped by first thing this morning. He seems to be doing fine. He didn't want to talk about how the doctor said he should be taking it easy, and when I teased him about the hospital food he didn't even rise to the bait. I was kind of disappointed." Amanda knew Lisa and Ethan had been friends for a long time, and was kind of disappointed that the flirting she'd seen between the two of them recently hadn't gone any further than it had.

"So, his concussion's better? That's good news. He was pretty loopy when I saw him at the hospital."

Lisa grabbed Finn before he could make a mad dash up the main stairway. "Seems good as new. He's actually kind of proud of the stitches he got. Says it's gonna make him look tough."

Meg scoffed. "What is it about guys and scars? Women hate scars and guys brag about them. I think men are weird."

Lisa pulled the little cat into her lap. "If you think men are so weird, then why even bother? Speaking of that, how's the internet dating going these days, Meg?"

"Oh, you know me," Meg said with a little laugh, her eyes carefully on the ornaments in her hands. "I'm always on the search for my next soon-to-be-ex-boyfriend." Amanda and Lisa exchanged a quick glance. They both knew that behind her happy exterior, Meg really wanted to be in a relationship. A couple of weeks before, Lisa and Amanda had made a quiet agreement to keep their eyes open for a nice guy for Meg.

"Have you heard anything else about the body you found? Last I heard they hadn't released a name or said anything about him being dug out. Are there any missing persons in this area?"

Amanda shook her head. "James couldn't tell me much, except that they finally got the body out from under the landslide and took it to the medical examiner. He said that nobody was listed as missing in Ravenwood Cove, and they checked around the area, in Likely and Morganville." She pulled out the individual blown glass ornaments, checking them for breakage, but her mind was obviously on what had happened earlier at the mudslide. "He said this guy may have been dead a couple of months."

Lisa looked surprised. "A couple of months and he wasn't reported missing? Kinda weird."

Carefully setting the ornaments back in the egg-crate box, Amanda shrugged. "I haven't had a chance to talk to James much in the last couple of days but I'm supposed to meet him at Heinrich's for pizza at six. Maybe he'll have some more news for us."

Apparently hearing the commotion, Oscar finally roused himself enough to stalk silently out of the kitchen and investigate what was happening in the parlor. A huge orange cat Amanda had saved from starvation, he definitely considered himself the official greeter of everyone who came in the front door of the Ravenwood Inn. Lisa tried to hold tightly onto her wriggling kitten, but as soon as Finn saw Oscar he was struggling to go meet him. The older cat, confident in his role as ruler of the entire building, gently touched noses with the tiny kitten and then flopped down at Lisa's feet, seemingly satisfied. Lisa glanced at Amanda and finally let Finn go. He headed straight for Oscar, touched noses with him again, and then crawled across his back to flop down in happy comfort. Lisa petted Oscar's head and he started to purr loudly, just the tip of his tail twitching as the gray kitten snuggled into his fur.

"Well, I guess he's not going to shred him, so that's a good thing," she sighed in relief. "Good boy, Oscar."

"Well, ladies, I've got to run." Meg pulled her coat off the brass rack by the door. "Gram should be done down at Petrie's and I've got to pick her up. Did I tell you Brian ran out of pickles and just gave her a bologna sandwich for lunch yesterday? I heard about it all the way home, and she insisted that we had to go buy more pickles so she could give them to him when she got there this morning."

Amanda smiled. No matter how much Meg might gripe about her opinionated grandmother, she knew that her friend loved her deeply. She had the difficult job of being both granddaughter and helper, whenever her grandmother needed assistance.

"Give her my love."

Meg shot Amanda a quick grin. "Will do."

Chapter 5

As usual, stepping into Heinrich's Pizzeria was like walking into a basil- and cheese-scented heaven. The buttery fragrance of freshly-baked dough and caramelized garlic lured in passersby, even if they didn't think they wanted pizza. For once, James was in the restaurant before Amanda walked in the door. She smiled, appreciating his punctuality. It seemed like he almost always showed up late due to something happening with his job as a detective, and this was a nice change.

"I already ordered a Breathbuster pizza," he said, grinning at her. "I figured you'd be hungry and I know what you like." He stood up and gave her a quick peck on the cheek and a squeeze of her hand before she slid into the padded booth.

"Extra cheese?"

"Of course. Before you say another word—" he said, his eyes sparkling with humor, "—I'll bet you a dollar I know what you're going to say. Or rather, what you're going to *ask*."

She suppressed a smile. "I have no idea what you mean," she lied. She knew darn well that he was aware she was meeting him so she could ask him questions about the body from the mudslide.

Amanda scanned the room quickly, noting that James had chosen a corner booth tucked away from the other patrons. There were only a few, since it was winter on the Oregon coast and the flow of tourists had

33

turned into a trickle. A young mother corralled two boisterous boys on the other side of the room, and a middle-aged couple dressed in matching rain jackets were quietly arguing with each other as they were dishing up the gooey pizza in front of them. Apparently Ian Victor, the owner of the local boat rental business, had given up on Ivy's Cafe, because he was sitting in the pizza parlor, reading his paper and drinking a huge mug of coffee. From the crumpled napkins around him, it looked like he'd been there for quite some time.

Sitting at the back was the tall tourist with the metal detector that Amanda had seen before at Cuppa. He was picking at a small salad and avoiding anyone's gaze. *Must be staying with family,* she thought, *since he's not staying at the Inn.*

James pulled out a small notebook and a steel pen, waiting. "You know the drill, lady. Most of this info is going to be in the papers anyway but I want to make sure that nobody, especially Lisa, hears about how he died or what we discovered in the autopsy. Deal?"

Amanda bristled a bit. Her friend, Lisa Wilkins, was editor of the local paper but that didn't mean Amanda went and blabbed everything that she'd heard to her. Sometimes it was a balancing act, dating a detective and having a friend who wanted to know about the hottest news stories, but Amanda was careful to keep her mouth shut. Maybe that was one of the reasons James trusted her so much.

"You know I can keep things confidential. I just feel like since I was the one who found the body, I should get to know who he was." She leaned forward. "I did touch his gross sock, after all."

"I know, but I still have to say it." James flipped the small notebook open. "First things first. The man's name was Desmond Martin. We were able to ID him from his dental records and confirmation from the new tattoo on his calf."

James continued, checking over his notes. "He used to work at the car wash over in Morganville and his coworkers say they haven't seen him in several months. He was twenty-six, lived alone, and had several things on his police record, but nothing recent."

Amanda's mind was whirling, thinking of what James had said. Knowing the dead man's name and a bit of his history made everything so much more real. She'd never even seen the man's face, just his two feet, but now that she knew where he'd lived and worked she could almost picture him in her mind's eye.

"What sort of things did he have on his record?"

"Petty theft, mostly. One bust for possession, one for arson."

"Does anyone know how he got on the hillside?"

James sighed. "He didn't get *on* that hillside. He got put *in* that hillside. Preliminary evidence shows that he was actually buried somewhere on that hill. Maybe at the top."

Amanda's mouth dropped open. "You mean he– "

James' eyes met hers. "He was murdered, Amanda. No doubt about it."

They sat in silence, digesting the news. James sighed. "We won't have all the results back for quite some time but he was shot in the head. Twice, at close range."

Suddenly, Amanda didn't feel so hungry anymore. Whatever Desmond Martin's past was, she couldn't help but feel sorry for a man who was murdered in such a terrible way. Being dumped in a makeshift grave and then having a mudslide spill his corpse across the rutted road was a horrible ending to a very young life.

"How awful." She suppressed a shudder. "So, that means someone in this area, probably, right? It had to be somebody close by who killed him."

James nodded. "It could've been somebody just moving through, a tourist or a drifter, but it could be somebody still close by." He took a quick sip of his coffee. "There's another thing. Martin had his pockets turned out. Someone was obviously looking for something. We have no way to know what it is was or whether the killer found it. The lab's trying to get an identification from the bullets that were recovered, but the last I heard they hadn't found anything in the databases. Right now, we don't know anything about the gun that killed him."

"But you know what caliber the bullet was, right?" Amanda had a sinking sense of déjà vu as she asked that question, remembering back to another conversation with James. The last time she'd asked that question, no one had actually been shot. They were just investigating bullet holes found in a boat that held a dead man.

This case was something entirely new. She didn't want to think about how they retrieved the bullets.

Just as James opened his mouth to answer her question, his cell phone buzzed. Picking it up, he checked the incoming text and his eyebrows raised. "I hate to do this," he said, "but I've got to go. Looks like you'll have to eat that pizza by yourself. I'll call you later."

Amanda felt a stab of disappointment as he kissed her on the cheek and squeezed her hand, before striding briskly out the door. Sometimes it seemed like his job came first, and she wished she was able to see more of him. She truly appreciated how hard he worked and how he protected the people in the little beach town that she loved, but she still would've liked to just have a simple conversation over a warm pizza.

Sighing, Amanda flagged down the waitress and asked if she could wrap up the food to take home with her. Maybe Oscar liked pepperoni.

Chapter 6

It wasn't normal to see a crowd of people in front of any of the display windows on Main Street, so Amanda was surprised at the group of people, seemingly transfixed, in front of the Bake Me Happy bakery. Standing under the pink- and white- striped awning, nearly a dozen townspeople were so absorbed in looking at the front window that nobody even noticed when Amanda walked up. Mrs. Mason, the owner, was standing outside with a huge grin on her face, answering questions from the crowd. Amanda craned her head to try to see around the people in front of her, and finally realized what everyone was gawking at. Bake Me Happy had just recently put in a new candy counter, complete with huge glass jars filled with different types of sweet treats, and apparently they decided to add saltwater taffy to their selection. There were several large, strange-looking machines in the window, all apparently for making salt water taffy. The one closest to the window was nearly mesmerizing to watch. It had two metal sets of arms that faced each other, and when Celia, Mrs. Mason's assistant, slid a fat loop of warm taffy over one set of the arms and switched the machine on, it began to rhythmically stretch and fold the gooey treat.

So, that's what they mean by a taffy pull, Amanda mused as she watched Celia dump the syrupy contents from a warm copper kettle onto a cornstarch-dusted marble slab. Mrs. Mason was outside, passing out samples of peppermint-striped taffy. She was happily telling anyone who would listen about how she'd made the bargain of the century when she'd bought the nearly-antique equipment from a retired candy maker in Grants Pass.

"Sixty years old and it still works as good as the day it was made," she crowed, making sure that the two children in the front of the crowd got their sample of candy. "You know, they *used* to make machinery to last." She pushed the front door of the bakery open and followed Amanda inside. "I'll bet those machines last another sixty years." Humming happily, she stepped behind the counter and quickly tied a clean, pink apron around her waist. "Now, what can I do for you, Amanda?" she asked.

Amanda scanned the glass jars and finally pointed at a canister of brightly-colored sweets. "Can I get a pound of this, please? I didn't know anyone still made old-fashioned ribbon candy anymore."

Mrs. Mason chuckled as she expertly scooped up the hard candy, made to look like pleated silk ribbons, and filled a small bag. "You'd be amazed at how many of the old types of candy still exist. You ever had a Squirrel Nut Zipper?"

"Um, isn't that the name of a band? Does hot swing music?"

Mrs. Mason folded over the top of the bag and tucked away the scoop. "Never heard of 'em. Maybe it is, but where do you think they *got* their name?" She stepped over to the bins of salt water taffy, each sorted by flavor. "How about some taffy?"

Amanda was still watching Celia. The younger woman's eyebrows were knit together in absolute concentration as she used two broad spatulas to maneuver the cooling candy on the slab. Ignoring the crowd who was still watching through the window, she set down the spatulas and then put the empty copper kettle on a nearby stand, before starting to measure cup after cup of sugar. Amanda had never seen anyone be so precise with their measuring or their cooking. Celia very slowly skimmed any extra grains of sugar off the top of the measuring cup with a broad frosting knife, then raised it up to her eye level to double check it again before dumping it into the copper pot.

"That girl seems pretty serious about her job, Mrs. Mason. She always this intense?"

Mrs. Mason peered over the top of her glasses, following Amanda's gaze. "Now, don't you go teasing about Celia. She had to figure out how to use the equipment from watching YouTube videos, and she's one of the best employees I've got. It's not like they had a lot of homemade taffy stores in Oklahoma. She's only been in town six months and I already don't know what I'd do without her. Between her and Dave, they practically run the store for me."

"I wasn't teasing about Celia, I promise! Must be nice to have an employee who is able to take over something new like that."

Mrs. Mason smiled at her. "Wait 'til you see the huge gingerbread house Dave's making for the Hometown Holidays display! It's amazing. Has windows made of melted candy and everything." Amanda knew Dave Barton had been a logger for a large foresting company until he was laid off recently, and it had taken a while for him to realize that his ability to make mouth-watering scones and rolls could get him a job at Bake Me Happy. Word around town was that he was much happier rolling out dough and fussing over a hot oven than he had been chopping down trees.

Amanda smiled at Mrs. Mason. "I'll stop by and check it out."

The plump lady smiled. "Peppermints?" At Amanda's answering nod, she scooped up some taffy into a bag, stopping when Amanda put up her hand.

"That's about a half a pound. By the way, heard anything about the mudslide guy?"

For some reason, Mrs. Mason's well-intended question rankled a bit. After hearing about how the man was a victim of a cold-blooded murder, it sounded almost disrespectful to have someone address him as 'the mudslide guy'.

Amanda suppressed her emotions and her voice was steady and calm. "I'm sure the papers will have more news soon." It wasn't exactly a lie. She couldn't pass along what James had told her and she was hoping that her vague response would satisfy Mrs. Mason.

Apparently not. Mrs. Mason's eyebrows raised in surprise. "Well, I'm sure they will," was all she said as she handed Amanda the bags of candy and turned to help the next customer.

A trip to Madeline Wu's fish store for smoked salmon, and a quick chat with the Hortman brothers as they were setting up a good-sized Christmas tree lot next to Petrie's hardware store, and Amanda had had enough excitement for one day. Time to go back to the Inn and get ready for her next batch of guests at the bed and breakfast.

Chapter 7

So much for the romance of decorating.

By the time she'd wrestled the freshly-cut holly branches into a thick plastic bag, Amanda was truly grateful that she was wearing heavy leather gloves and had brought a pair of long-handled kitchen tongs. The glossy green foliage and bright red berries would look wonderful on the carved mantle over the main fireplace, but after being poked repeatedly she was rethinking her brilliant idea. When she'd first thought about pruning her huge holly tree at the back corner of the Ravenwood Inn's acreage, she had no idea how tough it was going to be to avoid getting stabbed by countless little thorns. She was almost regretting taking advantage of the time her guests were gone, off to a local tour, but it gave her time to get her outdoor chores done, including gathering greenery to decorate.

No wonder nothing eats these leaves, she thought, gingerly pulling together the edges of the bag. *Not even the deer like a mouthful of ouch.*

Holding the sack of holly carefully in one hand, she picked up the wire egg basket with the other. There weren't as many eggs as there had been a few weeks ago. The hens had started molting, so that meant there were loose feathers blowing around the chicken coop, and the hens were laying fewer eggs. The first time Amanda had come outside to see a rumpled hen with bald patches and a naked tail she was sure that the poor bird had contracted some rare avian disease and would need a vet and maybe last rites. She didn't calm down until Jennifer had come over, because of her frantic phone call, and laughingly assured her that molting was a natural process and that the birds weren't infected with some dread disease.

Sometimes it wasn't easy being a transplanted city girl trying to live in a rural small town.

The only bird that hadn't been affected by molting was her multi-colored rooster, Dumb Cluck. He was still as gorgeous and loud as ever. His beady eyes watched her warily as she double checked the gate to be sure it was latched, and as she walked back toward the Inn. Even though he was loud and obnoxious, she made sure that he had a good, warm place to stay and all the healthy chicken feed he needed. Dumb Cluck was just a chicken, that's true, but he was also a hero. He had alerted her when the Inn had been set on fire, and that got him privileges for the rest of his days. Amanda was determined that he and his new harem of nearly-bald hens were going to have long, happy lives.

It was quite a walk back over several acres, and she could feel the chill seeping through her jacket. It was getting colder, that was for sure. Amanda had watched until there was a break in the drizzle, and timed her chores between rainclouds. According to the forecast, dry weather was on its way and that suited her fine. She missed seeing the unparalleled brilliance of diamond stars in a clear sky over the ocean, and was getting tired of having to take an umbrella everywhere she went. She'd just started to figure out that many townspeople were so used to the weather they just wore good raincoats with weatherproof hoods, and simply buttoned up when they stepped outdoors on a wet day.

By the time she'd reached the garden, she could make out a tall figure sitting on her back-kitchen porch, reading the latest copy of the Ravenwood Tide. Even with his face buried behind the broad pages of the newspaper, she'd have known those well-worn cowboy boots anywhere.

"Afternoon, Detective. What's new in the Tide?"

"Hmmmmmm. Hometown Holidays are coming up. Time to check that you have snow chains and good tires." He flipped the page. "Deep mulch can save your flower bed from freezing. The Catholic parish is having a live nativity scene on Saturday and Sunday. Ian Victor's bought a bigger boat and he's scheduling guided tours for whale watching, weather permitting. Oh, and the road to Likely has been cleared of mud and is now open."

Amanda set the egg basket and bag of holly down on the porch, settling into a wicker chair next to James. Thank goodness there was a deep overhang that protected it from most weather.

"Nothing about a murder, I take it?"

"Oh, that." He folded the newspaper carefully and held it out to her, front page on top. "Thought you'd already seen it."

The article was written by Lisa, and as so many of her articles were, was factual and clear. It detailed the discovery of the body, had basic information about Desmond Martin's job and where he lived. A small photo, probably from his Facebook profile, was set off to the side of the columns of text. There wasn't much beyond that, and Amanda could tell the police were doing their best to keep details about the victim's life and their investigation as private as possible.

Amanda studied the victim's picture. It might have been taken at a wedding, or a school dance, but the grainy photo told her very little about the short life of a man who'd met a terrible end. He was wearing a suit and smiling nervously in the photo, with carefully-combed hair and slightly crooked tie.

"Lisa didn't say anything about cause of death, just that foul play was suspected." She folded the newspaper and looked at James. "I take it you didn't tell her about the two bullets?"

The detective uncrossed his long legs and got up, reaching for the bag and basket. "We didn't give her details. The killer already knows how he died, and if anyone comes forward to talk to the investigators we need to know they actually have info that isn't just made up or something they read in the paper. People do that sometimes."

After the bracing cold of the outdoors, the Inn's kitchen was almost too warm. Earlier, Amanda had started a pot of chicken soup on low heat, and the steam added to the cozy atmosphere. Turning down the stove so the soup wouldn't boil, Amanda sighed as she stripped off the heavy leather work gloves and jacket.

"Want some coffee? I just made a fresh pot."

"That'd be great."

By the time she'd poured two mugs full and plopped down onto one of the chairs at the Inn's long harvest table, James had already corralled the little pitcher of cream from the fridge. From the pensive look on his face, Amanda could tell that he had something on his mind. Pouring the coffee, she asked, "So, what's new with you, James? You don't normally stop by so I'm guessing you have a reason."

"Maybe I just wanted a piece of leftover pizza."

"You're too late. Jennifer and I already split it." She smiled at him, waiting, until he finally came clean.

"Actually, I do have a reason. We got some more information back from the medical examiner and the investigation team. It turns out our victim was hiding a secret that he really didn't want to share."

"A secret? What kind of secret?" She could feel her heartbeat quicken, as it always did at the beginning of a really good mystery.

"He was hiding a key. We missed it on our first go-round, because it was hidden so well. It was actually sewn into the lining of his sneaker, under the padding. When we examined it we could tell that it had the info filed off the top. Whatever that brass key was for, Desmond Martin knew he had to hide it."

"So, do you think the person who turned out his pockets was looking for that key?"

James unzipped his jacket as he considered her question. "That would be my guess. No one would hide a key like that unless they were worried someone was going to find it. Mr. Martin obviously had a reason."

"Maybe that reason was what killed him."

James' face was grim. "Maybe it did."

"And there's no way to track the key? To find out what it goes to?"

"You ask a lot of questions, lady." James' grin was lopsided, but he pulled a folded piece of paper out of his back pocket, obviously prepared.

Unfolding it, he said, "Whatever was stamped on the metal has been filed off, as you can see, but the shape of the key itself is unusual. I did a bit of investigating on the shape and it doesn't appear to be any standard style of key. This one was probably custom made, and probably old."

Amanda leaned over the photocopied photo, intrigued. The picture was large and detailed, showing every scratch and groove in the old, brass key. The top of the key was worn smooth, but the outline was distinctive – four rounded lobes, with a hole punched at the very top so it could be hung on a chain or keyring. It looked old, the nicks in the grooved part that went in a lock showed its age and previous use, and there was a tarnish to the brass.

James tapped on the picture. "We're kind of at a dead end about the key. We don't know what lock it goes to, and we don't know why the victim wanted to hide it so bad. I'd be pretty sure that whatever he was trying to hide –"

"Or protect," Amanda interrupted him. "Maybe he was protecting something."

James looked thoughtful. "Maybe. Either way, we may never know. The bottom line is, he didn't want anyone to find it."

Amanda studied the photocopy again. "Is this your copy?"

"Doesn't have to be." When she looked up, Amanda could see the surprise in James' eyes. "You want to have a crack at figuring out this key?"

She paused. "Well, I've been talking with the ladies at the historical society a lot lately, trying to get info on the Inn. They've been really helpful about finding me old photos, and we get along well. Maybe someone there could point us in the right direction. It's at least worth a try."

James shrugged. "I can always print off another copy of the photo. It's yours, and just let me know if you find out anything. But Amanda," he paused until he had her full attention, "don't forget to use your good judgement. You're a sharp cookie, and I expect you to know when to stop. Promise?"

Folding the paper and tucking it into her pocket, Amanda laughed. "I promise. I'll use good sense."

Chapter 8

"I want a smartphone. I've already told Meg I wanted one for Christmas," Mrs. Granger said, putting her purse on the table.

Amanda paused, a box of cornstarch in her hand, the cabinet door in Mrs. Granger's kitchen still open. Her ninety-year-old friend had her arms crossed across her chest, a look of absolute determination on her face.

"Why would you want a smartphone? You have trouble operating your home phone."

"Don't be cheeky, young lady," Mrs. Granger huffed in disapproval. "I'm not too old to learn, am I?" Sitting on the sturdy plastic seat of her walker, she shook a finger at Amanda. "I have as much right to be on the innerweb as anyone. I could figure out how to use The Google. Besides," she finally smiled a bit, "Meg says these days they have all sorts of games on phones that I'd like. I used to be quite a poker player in my day, you know."

Amanda kept putting the groceries away. Meg hadn't been able to drive her grandmother to the store for her usual Tuesday shopping trip due to a dentist appointment, so Amanda had volunteered. She always enjoyed spending time with her opinionated ninety-year-old friend, and she'd needed to get supplies for the Inn anyway.

"I'll bet you were. Who taught you to play poker, Mrs. Granger?"

"Hubert did," she replied, referring to her long-dead husband. "My daddy used to play with friends at our house when I was growing up, but he never thought it was right that a girl would play gambling games like that. Said it wasn't proper." She smiled. "Hubert didn't worry about stuff like that so much."

"I think I would've liked Hubert." Amanda carefully folded the paper bags and tucked them into the small pantry. Every shelf was crammed full of saved foil, recycled string, grocery sacks, and rows of home-canned food.

"You ever going to clean this pantry out?" Amanda asked. "I could help. How many rubber bands do you really need?" She picked up a Mason jar, full of twisted bands in all colors.

Mrs. Granger looked over the top of her glasses. "My, aren't we just uppity today. Didn't your Mama ever teach you the little poem 'use it up, wear it out, make it do or do without'?"

"I can't say she did." Amanda thought back to how hard her mother had worked to make a living for the two of them, and the solitary holidays where her mother was busy working at the hospital. Amanda had spent a lot of time on her own when she'd lived with her Mom, and she'd certainly never heard her give advice about making do. It was just a reality in their house, and one of the reasons Amanda had worked so hard to get through college. She wanted more of a life than her worried and eternally-tired mother seemed to have.

Mrs. Granger continued. "Well, my Mama did. She lived through the Great Depression and two World

Wars, and she taught me the importance of being thrifty. It's gotten me through some very tough times. Now," she said, apparently wanting to change topics, "what's going on with the murder investigation? There isn't squat in the papers that's new."

Amanda looked at her ancient friend, considering. Out of all the people she knew, Mrs. Granger was the most knowledgeable and certainly one of the best historians for the area. James had cautioned her against divulging details of the state of Desmond Martin's body or the way he was killed, but he'd given her permission to ask some questions from the local historical society.

It was an easy decision.

"Actually, the investigation's kind of bogged down, and maybe you could help. Would you mind if I showed you something, and see if you recognized it?"

The old lady grinned. "I'd be happy to. James know you're showing me stuff?"

Amanda smiled and dug through her purse for the folded piece of paper James had given her. "Who's being uppity now? You know I wouldn't compromise his investigation."

"I know, but I just had to ask." Mrs. Granger seemed wholly unrepentant. She watched as Amanda smoothed the sheet of paper onto the kitchen tabletop.

Leaning over, the old lady adjusted her spectacles a bit as she examined the blown-up image of the key that had been found sewn in Desmond Martin's shoe.

"Lucky Rail."

Amanda's heart stopped. "What?"

"It's a Lucky Rail key. I'd bet my boots on it." She straightened up with a smile of satisfaction on her lined face. "My husband used to work at the local depot, loading cargo. I'd know that logo anywhere. Lucky Rail had everything marked with their four-leaf clover design, even the keys."

"Are you sure?"

Mrs. Granger shot Amanda a look of disgust. "Didn't I just say I was? That's a railroad key. Might've gone to the depot door or some box they used on the trains when it ferried stuff back and forth through here."

"I didn't know Ravenwood Cove had a railroad that went through here."

"We don't now, but we used to have one. Lots of farmers sent their milk and produce to the big towns by rail, and the fishermen used to get the best price for sending oysters and fish that way, too. It used to be the roads around here were really rough, and the railroad was the fastest and easiest way to ship things."

Amanda was stunned. She should've know that Ravenwood Cove's oldest resident, who'd made it her business to know what was going on with everyone in town, would've been a goldmine of information when it came time to figure out a mysterious key.

"Is Lucky Rail still around?"

The sound Mrs. Granger made with her pursed lips wasn't very ladylike. "Not for decades. When the roads improved the railroads weren't as necessary, and Ravenwood Cove was just a little spur line anyway. Our town didn't even make it on the scenic tourist train route that runs along the coast. When Lucky Rail closed up shop, Hubert was left without a job for a while, until he finally started up with the logging company. He didn't even get his last paycheck when the railroad shut down."

A dead end.

"Mrs. Granger, why would a young man have a key belonging to a defunct railroad?"

The elderly lady was obviously thinking over her answer. "Well, I think it would be one of two things. Either he got that key from someone who used to work for the railroad, or maybe he's been snooping around the property the railroad used. Lucky Rail left some equipment and things around here when they closed down, so maybe he was going through the stuff around and found the key."

Amanda leaned forward, her eyes intent on her ninety-year-old companion. "Left some things where? What sort of things?"

Mrs. Granger shrugged. "Well, the abandoned tracks and the depot. That's the only thing I can think that would be left. It's north of town a few miles. It hasn't been used in at least... I don't know how many years, but if you wanted to find out something about this key I recommend you start there."

Amanda didn't remember seeing a depot, but if Mrs. Granger said it was in the area, it must be there.

The old lady pulled a plastic bag of paper napkins out of the grocery bag, still thinking. "There used to be another depot in Morganville, but squatters set it afire about a year ago. I think Ravenwood's the only Lucky Rail depot for miles around." She pulled out the drawer to the sideboard and put the napkins away. "They would've used several locks at the depot." She started ticking them off on her fingers. "The front door, the cargo door, the stationmaster's office. My husband was kind of a packrat, bless his heart, and he never threw anything away. I know he had some stuff left when they closed the depot down, his whistle and keys and such, and I know he had a key. I think it went to the cargo room." She looked around, as if searching for something. "He said it was the least they could give him since they never gave him his last paycheck. I'd bet that Lucky Rail key is still on his big, old keyring. I think it's still in his desk in the office. Might not be exactly the same as the one in the photo, but it might be able to get you in one of the doors."

She pushed her walker ahead of her, leading the way to the tiny office at the back of her house. It was crammed with books and file cabinets, with a small roll top desk wedged in one corner. Amanda watched from the doorway while Mrs. Granger methodically started going through the drawers, rooting around and muttering to herself as she searched for Hubert's hoarded keys. Occasionally, she'd find a piece of paper that she'd examine and stuff in her pocket, apparently to be perused later. After several long minutes, she finally extracted a huge wad of keys on an oversized, homemade ring. She flipped through a few of them, then gave a sigh of exasperation and used both hands to give the heavy bundle to Amanda.

"See what I mean about him being a packrat? I think there are still keys on there from our first Chevy."

Amanda turned on a desk lamp and started examining the keyring. It didn't take long for her to find the sole Lucky Rail key that Hubert had saved. The four-leaf clover shape definitely stood out. It took a bit of wrangling, but after a few minutes she was able to extract the key off the wire ring.

"That's it." There was a sound of satisfaction in Mrs. Granger's voice, and she was pleasantly surprised when Amanda leaned over and gave her resounding peck on the cheek.

"Mrs. Granger, you are a wonder. May I borrow this key? I'd like to go check out the depot."

The old lady's eyebrows went up. "Check this out without me? Are you crazy? I was the one who gave you that clue. Besides," she said, rubbing her hands together in anticipation, "I'd love to see the depot again. It's been locked up tight and I haven't been there in years. I used to drive down and take Hubert a hot lunch pail every day."

The thought of Mrs. Granger being her sleuth sidekick was ludicrous. The old lady relied completely on her walker to get around, and even though she was incredibly sharp of mind, Amanda couldn't stomach the thought of her being involved in a murder investigation. Sometimes, things didn't go well and it could be dangerous for the old lady. Amanda had grown to love her, almost as if she were her own grandmother.

Besides, she knew Meg would kill her if she took Mrs. Granger with her. Beneath Meg's sweet blonde exterior was someone who would do anything to protect the people she loved. The idea of having her mad at Amanda wasn't a pleasant prospect.

Amanda made up her mind. "I'm sorry, but I don't think that's a good idea. You never know what can happen when you're investigating something like this."

Mrs. Granger crossed her arms, her lips a thin line of defiance. "Well, if you really thought this was so dangerous you'd be calling James to go with you, and I haven't heard you say a word about *that*." She smiled smugly. "I promise I'll watch your back."

"I think it's a bad idea."

Mrs. Granger's tone became wheedling. "Amanda, I'm overdue for some adventure and at my age, what do I have to lose?"

Amanda patiently explained her reasoning. "I don't need James to go with me because all I'm doing is checking if this key works on any of the doors at the depot. That's it. I'm not risking my safety, and I'm certainly not going to risk yours."

"Then give me back my key."

"Are you kidding?'"

The stony face of her stubborn companion plainly showed she wasn't kidding at all. "I'm a full-grown adult with all my faculties and I want to go with you to the depot."

57

By the steely glint in Mrs. Granger's eyes, Amanda knew she just lost the argument. If she wanted to use the key, she'd have to take the old lady with her. Resigned, she picked up her coat and stuffed her arms into the sleeves. "Fine, but if Meg's mad about this, I'm blaming you."

"Deal!" Mrs. Granger clapped her hands together in glee. "I call shotgun."

Chapter 9

All the way to the depot, Amanda gripped the steering wheel tightly and tried to keep from muttering swear words under her breath. This was a bad idea. A terribly bad idea. An idea that should be spanked and sent to bed early sort of an idea.

She should never have told Mrs. Granger she could come with her. The old lady was nearly bouncing in her seat, humming happily and pointing out areas of interest to Amanda as they drove past. Most of her stories seemed to revolve around other people and their love lives, and after Amanda had heard the second tale about which couple had been discovered naked under which big tree while they were courting, her patience had almost snapped.

By the time Mrs. Granger had pointed out the nearly-overgrown entry to the depot's parking lot, Amanda was looking forward to leaving the older lady in the car. With an assurance to Mrs. Granger that she'd be right back, Amanda got out and pulled up the hood on her coat. Even though the sun wasn't completely set yet, the darkness under the high canopy of the fir tree forest seemed to block out much of the light. Hanging moss and lichens on the black-trunked trees lent an air of foreboding to the whole area.

Not exactly Disneyland, she thought, as she gave a short wave of goodbye to Mrs. Granger. The old lady seemed pretty ticked off. She had her arms crossed, and was having an angry, muttered conversation with herself as she was sitting alone in the car.

Amanda turned toward the depot, pulling out her flashlight. *Can't be helped that she's mad at me,* she thought resignedly. *I'll just have to apologize later. Might need a couple of boxes of doughnuts to smooth over her feathers a bit.*

The depot was just a short walk from the car but Amanda had to pick her way through the fallen branches and pieces of forest debris that were scattered all over the parking lot. A quick scan of the area and she instantly realized that she'd parked in the one spot that was clear. A spot that was exactly the size of a parked car.

Someone had been here before, and someone had made sure they had a place to park.

She gripped the flashlight more tightly. A little voice in the back of her brain was telling her that she should wait, and that she should call the police. She'd heard that voice in the past and she knew it meant she needed to be extra cautious. Looking around, the place seemed completely abandoned. There was no place to hide another vehicle. She stood still for a few moments, straining her ears, but only heard the dripping of the wet trees and the rustle of birds moving.

The small depot building stretched parallel to the abandoned railroad tracks. Large sheets of weathered plywood were nailed over the windows, and a bright orange NO TRESPASSING sign had been attached to the siding. It looked like there was an office on one end and a cargo area with a raised platform and barn door on the other. The center section had a sign over the single door that said PASSENGERS, apparently leading to the waiting room where tickets would have been purchased.

Amanda tried turning the slick doorknob for the passenger section but it didn't budge. She pulled out the Lucky Rail key and it was cold in her hand as she inserted it and carefully tried to turn the bolt. Nothing. The key didn't work in the lock at all. Amanda felt a stab of disappointment that she couldn't get it to move. The entrance was locked up tight.

Even though she knew she was alone, Amanda kept glancing around her as if she was going to be grabbed by someone demanding to know why she was trying to get into the depot. Walking around the side of the building, she walked up the ramp to the cargo area. There was a raised platform for loading items onto the train, and a huge barn door for moving boxes and goods in and out of the storage area. She leaned timidly around the next corner, peering down the side of the building by the tracks, but there wasn't a soul in sight.

Time to try to get into the cargo area.

She pulled on the sliding barn door but it wouldn't budge, no matter how hard she tried. There was a normal-sized door at the side, and Amanda's hands were trembling a bit when she pulled out the Lucky Rail key again. Glancing around again, she took a deep breath and slid it into the door lock. It took a bit of maneuvering to get it all the way in, but when she tried to turn it the old lock it wouldn't budge. She set her shoulder against the door and tried her best to rotate the key but after several minutes of shoving and twisting as hard as she could, she finally gave up. The key she had didn't belong to the lock for the cargo room.

Amanda fumbled with her flashlight and shined it on the lock, instantly realizing that it wasn't nearly as old as the key in her hand. The shiny lock looked brand new, nothing like the tarnished lock on the front passenger area door.

She really didn't want to break anything to get in, and after trying that door she wasn't certain she could. A bit more snooping and when she walked back toward the parking lot she saw another door on the far end of the small building. There was a faded sign painted on the door, reading STATIONMASTER'S OFFICE. She was certain that Mrs. Granger was watching her, unless she'd dozed off, as she tried the key in the deadbolt lock. After a bit of wrangling with the stiff mechanism, she was nearly ready to give up entirely when suddenly the bolt slammed back, making her jump at the sudden sound.

Amanda checked her flashlight again, and holding it in front of her like a weapon, she put her hand on the knob and slowly pushed open the creaky wooden door.

It was dark as a cave inside until Amanda's light spilled into the room. Dust motes hung suspended in the cold air, as if frozen in time. For a split second, she hesitated at the doorframe. She'd never liked darkness, always being one of those kids who was scared to look in her nighttime closet in case something was looking back at her. Stepping inside, she scanned the room quickly. No monsters here. At least none she could see.

There was a broad, wooden desk and an old-fashioned rolling office chair in the corner of the room. A glass light fixture hung from the center of the ceiling, and a roll-up ticket window, probably leading to the small waiting room, was shut tight. A rusty four-drawer file cabinet sat next to the desk, the bottom drawer hanging open by a couple of inches. An old calendar was thumbtacked on the wall, next to a curled copy of a long-defunct train schedule.

The wooden floorboards squeaked a bit when she walked in, and the harsh sound was jarring, as if it announced her presence. It seemed wrong to be making noise in this abandoned place, as if someone would hear that she'd broken the seal on the outer door of a tomb. She flipped the light switch. Nothing. She'd known there was no electricity to the small building, but she'd had to try anyway.

But she hadn't broken the seal. Someone else had.

Shining her light on the desk, Amanda could see that the dust on the top had been scuffed and disturbed in several places. She pulled on the bottom of the desk drawer, feeling the resistance of the small lock. Focusing her flashlight on the keyhole, she could see that it appeared to be identical to the type of deadbolt that had been on the office door.

If the lock belonged to Lucky Rail, then there's a chance the key Desmond Martin had in his shoe might fit it, she thought.

After a few minutes of twisting her key in as hard as she could, she was puffing with exertion and nowhere nearer to opening the stubborn drawer.

Built to last, she thought in frustration. *Unfortunately.*

She shone her flashlight around the small room, searching for some sort of tool that would help her. Amanda brushed the hair out of her face as she opened the squeaky drawers of the lone file cabinet, finally striking pay dirt in the bottom drawer. There were several old tools in there, including a heavy screwdriver with a wooden handle.

Wedging the flat head of the screwdriver into the space between the top of the drawer and the desk, she wiggled it forward a bit and finally pushed upward as hard as she could. At first there was no progress at all, but as she gave a last-ditch effort and leaned all her weight forward on the handle, there was a loud crack of splitting wood. The stubborn drawer finally popped open, the broken wood splintering around the still-intact lock, and papers inside sliding a bit from the sudden movement.

Amanda grabbed her flashlight and shined it inside the drawer, pulling out pieces of paper and scanning them. They didn't appear to be anything but printed memos and old timetables; certainly nothing worth hiding a key in someone's shoe. Disappointed, she pulled the drawer out as far as it could go, probing toward the back and hoping desperately that no spiders had taken up residence inside.

Nothing but papers and long-abandoned pencils. Even with her heart pounding from excitement, Amanda could feel a wave of disappointment wash over her. This wasn't what Desmond Martin had been hiding.

Amanda gave a deep sigh and tried to push the wooden drawer back inside the old desk, but she'd pulled it out so far that it wasn't straight and it didn't slide back easily. Maneuvering it from side to side didn't seem to help much, so she finally pulled the entire thing out so she could line it up properly. She had it in place and was ready to shove it back into the desk when her fingers brushed against something under the drawer.

Something *taped* under the drawer.

Something that would be hidden by the wooden case around it when the drawer slid in, and that wouldn't be seen if the drawer was pulled out.

She yanked again, not realizing that she was barely breathing as she turned the drawer over.

There was a small, dark velvet bag duct taped to the bottom. It was no bigger than her palm, but whatever was in it was something that someone was trying to keep hidden.

Amanda laid the drawer upside down on the desk and carefully pulled the wide gray tape off the wood. She was barely breathing. Something shifted inside the bag with a delicate click. Loosening the drawstring, she upended the small bit of velvet over her open palm, and something beautiful spilled into her hand.

A necklace, but not a normal necklace. This piece of exquisite artwork was crafted from swirled bits of silver metal, probably platinum, wrapped around brilliant cut stones. Amanda's hand was shaking as she pulled on the chain, lifting the necklace so she could see what it truly looked like. Putting down the fabric bag, she grabbed the flashlight and shone it directly on the amazing piece of jewelry.

It was heavy with filigreed metal and the three perfect stones that dangled from the center, each as large as her fingernail. They reflected the light from her trembling flashlight beam with a brilliant blue-white sparkle, filling the room with dappled spots of color and leaping light. Instantly, Amanda knew that they were high-quality diamonds. Nothing else would shine like that, and their cut and color added to their beauty. She'd never seen anything so beautiful in her life, and suddenly realized that there must've been a very good reason that Desmond Martin didn't want anyone else to find his treasure. This was the sort of necklace that people fought over, bartered fortunes over, and apparently died over.

With that realization, Amanda was able to look at the diamonds in a less romantic light. This stunning necklace, so dazzling in her hand, had gotten someone killed.

Somehow the fabulous stones didn't seem to sparkle quite as brightly as they had just a second before. She carefully folded the necklace and slid it back into the velvet bag, then dropped it into her coat pocket. With no cell coverage in this area, she'd have to call James as soon as she got to a spot her phone would work. Amanda would make sure to tell him all about how she'd gotten it, and what she'd touched and what she'd moved. She knew his team would go through the stationmaster's office with a fine-toothed comb, but she wasn't going to risk anyone else taking the necklace, even if it was only left in the depot until James could drive over to retrieve it. Definitely would be much safer with her.

She shone her flashlight around the office once more, checking if there was anything else she needed to report. When the beam of light landed on an interior door, also with a lock in it, she paused. The passenger lounge was probably on the other side of the wall, since that was where the shuttered ticket window was.

Amanda pulled out the Lucky Rail key Mrs. Granger had given her and slid it gingerly into the lock, hoping it wouldn't get stuck. It went in perfectly and when she turned it, she could feel a deadbolt giving way. Grabbing her flashlight, she turned the doorknob and slowly pushed the squeaking wooden door open.

The quiet room was full of long wooden benches, as if it still waited for passengers to come sit and wait, clutching their handbags and eager to board the passenger coaches that would be coming any minute. There was another door on the far wall, with a small sign that read CARGO. Another lock, another attempt at moving the bolt, and to her surprise it turned. Apparently, the stationmaster key opened all interior door locks, but what Amanda saw when she pushed open the cargo door made her catch her breath in shock.

Someone had been in this room, and very recently, it appeared. There was a full-sized mattress set directly on the floor, with a camping lantern standing on a wooden box next to it, along with several half-burned candles and a couple of scattered candy bar wrappers. The makeshift bed was covered with thick comforters and a pair of pillows. A nearby chair had a pair of gloves on it and a red and green hand-knit scarf was laid across the top. A wooden broom was standing in the corner by a pile of dust and leaves that someone had swept up, and an empty wine bottle lay on its side on the bare plank floor.

Amanda shivered. Someone had been here, and it looked like someone definitely planned to come back. The room seemed suddenly too cold and too dark. Just as she took one more step into the space, there was a scuffling sound in the corner and a loud thump as something fell over and hit the wooden floor. Someone or something was in the room with her! She spun around and pulled the creaking door shut behind her, running across the waiting room and through the little office. Back outside, she didn't stop. The light was nearly completely gone now, the towering trees just looming pieces of darkness penning her in, and she clutched the little velvet bag with both hands as she ran back to the car. Sidestepping the fallen branches littering the parking lot, she took a big gulp of air as she finally grabbed the car's door handle, her heart still hammering in fear, her mouth dry.

"Well? Find out anything while you were out snooping around by yourself? You should've taken me with you, young lady. I know that depot like the back of my hand, I've been there so many times."

Amanda dropped the bag with the necklace into the cup holder between the front seats and pulled out her keys, frantically flipping through them until she found the car key. Jamming it into the ignition, the engine roared to life and she jerked the car into reverse, then forward as she accelerated out of the dark parking lot, the depot getting smaller and smaller in her rearview mirror.

It wasn't until they were around the second bend about a half mile later that Amanda took a deep breath and looked at Mrs. Granger. Her friend's mouth was set in a thin, hard line of defiance and she had crossed both arms over her chest.

"I can handle myself in a fight, you know. Never had any problems in the past and you'd be surprised at some of the stories I could tell. And why are you driving like a bat outta hell?" the old lady grumped.

Amanda kept driving as she gestured to the little bag.

"That's why."

A look of surprise crossed Mrs. Granger's face and she picked up the bag, weighing it in one hand. Opening the drawstring, she hooked a finger under the platinum chain and pulled the exquisite necklace free. Even in the darkness of the car, the trio of diamonds still sparkled with unholy light, and Mrs. Granger gasped.

"Holy cats!"

Amanda nodded, her eyes still on the road. "Yeah, you said it. Beautiful, isn't it?"

Her anger gone, Mrs. Granger turned the necklace a bit, peering at the large stones.

"Moonlight."

Cutting a glance sideways, Amanda could just make out Mrs. Granger's face, smug and satisfied.

"What?"

"I'd bet my bonnet that this is Mrs. Welch's missing diamond necklace. Her husband, God rest his soul, gave it to her years ago and told her it was an old family heirloom. Said it actually had been named Moonlight because of the way it glowed." She turned the necklace over again and, seemingly satisfied, carefully put it back in the velvet bag.

The old lady's eyebrows were knit together in concentration. "Where did you find it?"

"Taped under an old desk drawer, in that bag. Someone was definitely trying to hide it, and they did a pretty good job."

Amanda had been around Mrs. Granger enough to be able to tell when she was mulling over something.

"Why would someone bother to hide it? It's been missing for months. Why wouldn't they just sell it outright? Even if they pried the diamonds out and just sold those by themselves it would be worth thousands."

The old lady had a point. A random thief would've probably just hacked it up and sold off the pieces so they could get easy cash. She glanced at Mrs. Granger, seeing the look of puzzlement on her lined face.

Amanda knew the answer. "They couldn't sell it if they were already dead."

Mrs. Granger looked at Amanda, and her eyes lit up. "And they took the secret of its location with them to the next world."

Desmond Martin. A disguised key hidden in his shoe, and dead a couple of months.

They rode in silence for several minutes before Mrs. Granger spoke up.

"You *are* going to tell James about this, aren't you?"

Amanda paused. "Tell him about the necklace or the fact that I found it in a dark room in an abandoned depot?"

Mrs. Granger's silence hung between them, answering her question. Amanda sighed.

"Don't worry. I promise to tell him. As soon as we get into town I'll stop and text him."

Mrs. Granger fished Amanda's cell phone out of her purse. "I can do it. If I'm gonna have a smartphone I need to learn how to use it." She squinted at the locked screen.

"What number do I call to send James a text? Is it on the innerweb?"

Chapter 10

When Amanda contacted James to meet her outside of Ivy's Cafe, she already knew she was probably going to get a lecture. She'd known he wasn't going to be happy about her snooping around without him, so she'd already taken Mrs. Granger home. It took a bit of maneuvering to help the old lady out of her car and get her walker, but Amanda didn't mind. She made sure Mrs. Granger got into her snug little cottage safely, much to the lady's absolute disgust.

"I'm part of this team and you're sending me to the showers!"

Amanda had set Mrs. Granger's ancient black purse down on the kitchen table. "You know what he's going to say. You really want to be there when he says it to me?"

Mrs. Granger blinked at her, obviously considering. She'd known James for years, and had even been his after-school babysitter for a while. After all that time, she knew his personality well. It took a couple of seconds before she backtracked. "You're right. I don't want to be anywhere near that conversation. Best of luck to you, young lady," she added, as she pushed her walker toward the stove to make tea.

Summarily dismissed, Amanda had driven to Ivy's and waited patiently outside, occasionally running the heater in her car. It was less than ten minutes from her text to the time her passenger door was being yanked open and all six foot plus of a concerned detective folded himself into the car seat next to her.

"I thought we talked about you being careful." His eyes were locked on hers, his face showing irritation.

"We did, and I was."

"Going to an abandoned building to snoop through it isn't being careful. It's being reckless." His voice changed, suddenly less official-sounding. "You know better, Amanda. It's not your job to risk yourself. That's *my* job."

Frustrated, she tried to explain. "Look, I checked to be sure there was no one else at the depot when I was there. I was careful. There was nowhere else they could've hidden a car."

"What if they had a partner who'd left them at the depot while they went to get supplies? What if they'd come by bike or walked there? What if they'd had someplace to hide a car that you didn't know about?"

She thought it over and grudgingly had to agree that he had a point.

"You okay?" He wasn't looking at Amanda, but she could hear the fatigue and worry in his voice.

Of all the things he could've said, she hadn't expected that.

"Yeah, I'm fine." She took a deep breath. "I'll be more careful next time."

"Make sure there isn't a next time," he said, obviously trying to be calm. "Okay, so what did you find out?

She reached over and gently grabbed his wrist, turning the palm upward, and then set the velvet bag on his open hand. He frowned with concentration as he slowly opened the bag and peered inside, finally dumping the contents out. The delicate filigree and sparkling gemstones seemed out of place in his large hands.

Amanda gestured toward the necklace. "I found a key like the one in the photocopied picture you gave me. When I went to the depot— "

He closed his eyes and rubbed the bridge of his nose, his eyebrows furrowed as if in sudden pain. "Tell me everything, and don't leave anything out."

"Headache?" Amanda asked, helpfully.

Deep sigh. "No thanks, I already have one." He sighed again and opened his eyes.

"Okay, lady, start at the beginning, and don't leave anything out."

Chapter 11

It was a couple of days before James had time to swing by the Ravenwood Inn and update Amanda on what was new with the Desmond Martin case, and what was going to happen with the necklace. When he knocked on the front door and popped his head inside, the detective could hear Amanda's voice. He followed the sound to the kitchen, but what he saw there made him burst into laughter. Amanda was elbows-deep in a big bowl of gingerbread dough, seeming to struggle with the thick, gooey mass. Her expression reflected her frustration.

"Have a seat. I'd offer you coffee but I don't think I can get my hands out of this."

He tried to keep a straight face as he plopped onto a chair at the marble kitchen island. "First time making gingerbread cookies?"

Amanda looked disgusted. "Practically my first time making *any* cookies. I followed the recipe, but I didn't expect it to fight back." She carefully pried her hands out of the dough and wiped them on a couple of paper towels. "There might still be one of my rings in there."

He laughed. "Don't worry, somebody'll probably find it later."

"So, what brings you by?" she asked, rinsing her hands under the running tap. "It can't be my baking skills."

Reaching into his pocket, James extracted a very familiar-looking velvet bag. "The powers that be decided that the necklace didn't need to be kept as evidence, since it wasn't directly part of the murder, as far as we can tell."

"So, what happens to it now?" Amanda's eyebrows went up.

"I thought maybe you'd like to go with me to return it to Mrs. Welch. Technically, you're the finder of the necklace, and I think she posted a reward for it."

Amanda grimaced. "I can't just keep it?" She giggled when she saw James' seemingly-shocked expression. "I'm just kidding. Well, maybe I'm kidding. It *is* kind of stunning." She tried to keep a note of wistfulness out of her voice.

"Don't make me arrest you for theft, lady. Come on. You'll feel better about this whole thing if you get to see Mrs. Welch's face when we tell her we have her missing family heirloom."

"Okay, but give me a minute to get this goop off my hands first."

***

It turned out that Amanda had driven by Mrs. Welch's large house many times, but had never known who lived there. The imposing Craftsman home was near the edge of town, and flanked by a pair of massive oak trees and a scruffy lawn. Amanda pulled into the cracked concrete driveway behind an older-model pickup with a large sign on the side that read **SOLOMON CULPEPPER, Handyman At Large**.

As Amanda leaned over to open her car door, James put a hand on her arm and handed her the small velvet bag with the necklace inside. "You give it to her."

She could feel the stones shift in her hand and nodded. It was the right thing to give it back to the true owner.

Apparently, someone could hear them walk up the sidewalk. A disembodied voice came from underneath the house.

"Um, I'll be right out, Mrs. Sandford. Just about got the little sucker. I can see his beady little eyes from here."

Amanda turned to James, her eyebrows raised. Mrs. Sandford? What would the former mayor be doing at Mrs. Welch's house?

There was a lot of thumping and scuffling sounds, a couple of muttered exclamations, and then silence. James and Amanda glanced at each other, and then saw a pair of boot-covered feet slowly backing out from underneath the old house. It took a couple of minutes for the dust-covered handyman to emerge completely. Clasped in his right hand was a large gray squirrel, who was twitching his tail and looking very put out.

Struggling to his feet, the man seemed startled to see other people. He patted his coveralls ineffectively, trying to get off some of the dirt.

"Oh, hello. Sorry, thought you were Mrs. Sandford waiting to talk to me. She was wanting me to do some work out back of her art gallery this week."

Amanda pointed at the squirrel, her face reflecting her concern. "You're not going to kill it, are you?" Amanda loved watching the squirrels at the Inn. She knew some people considered them vermin, but the thought of the little creature, so frightened in the handyman's grip, being killed just seemed wrong.

Solomon snorted. "Not likely. Just need to put some new screens on the vents under Mrs. Welch's house so this little guy doesn't try to make it his winter hideaway again, that's all. Plenty of other places he can make into a home. I scooped out most of the acorns he'd hidden down there, so he's in good shape for the next few months." He thrust the squirrel at Amanda. "Care to hold him while I install the screens? Otherwise, he'll just go right back to where he was before."

Amanda jumped back a bit as Solomon waved the squirrel at her, the brushy tail swishing from side to side.

James stepped in, trying not to laugh out loud at Amanda's startled expression. "I've got a cardboard box in the back of my car and I can punch some air holes in it. I think that should hold the little guy until you're done with the vents. That work for you?"

At the handyman's nod, James headed back to his car to get the box, leaving Amanda standing with Solomon. Feeling apologetic, she tried to explain. "It's not that I don't like squirrels. I just didn't expect to have to hold one, that's all. Sorry if I flinched a bit."

Solomon chuckled, a smile crinkling the middle-aged lines around his eyes. "Don't worry about it, Miss. I'm pretty careful around wild critters myself. Don't want him to get the wrong idea and take a bite outta me."

With the squirrel safely stashed in James' box and sent off with Solomon to be rehomed, they were finally able to go up the wooden steps to the front door.

Looking around, Amanda realized that the beautiful old house hadn't been painted for years. The borders were carefully weeded and trimmed and the steps were swept clean, but that was where the maintenance ended. There was a crack in the glass of one of the front door panels that had been temporarily repaired by a wide piece of packing tape, and the doorbell was hanging by a single screw and a couple of bare wires.

Deciding not to mess with the dangerous-looking doorbell, Amanda knocked on the wood door. She stepped back politely and waited for someone to appear, but when no one opened the door she glanced at James, who shrugged. She knocked again, more forcefully, and within a minute or so they could hear the bolt in the lock being pushed back.

A thin woman, probably in her mid-fifties, cracked open the door to the full extent of the door chain and peered out at them.

Her eyes flicked between the two people on her porch. "Oh, I thought you were Hortense again. Be just a second," she said, and after that odd remark she shut the door again with a bang. There were the sounds of scrabbling as she unlatched the chain, and then she opened the door just wide enough to squeeze her slender frame through and shut it behind her. Standing squarely in front of the shut door, she put a hand up to her graying hair nervously, then turned toward the tall detective.

James, ever the gentleman, pulled off his hat. "Good afternoon, Mrs. Welch. I hope we didn't disturb you too much by coming by today."

The lady looked up at James, and Amanda could see a bit of hesitation on her face. "No, not at all. What can I do for you, Detective?" she asked, glancing at Amanda.

"This is my friend, Amanda Graham. She owns the Ravenwood Inn and she brought you something we thought you'd want to see."

Without a word, Amanda pulled the small velvet bag out of her coat pocket. The instant Mrs. Welch saw the little sack she went pale and she placed one hand on her heart.

"Is that...is that what I think...?"

Amanda loosened the strings and turned it over, spilling the brilliant treasure of the necklace into her cupped hand.

Mrs. Welch's fingers were trembling as she cautiously reached toward the necklace.

"Oh, dear Moonlight." There was a depth of sorrow in her simple exclamation, but the tremulous smile she gave Amanda showed her true feelings. Clasping the chain in both hands, she finally grinned, the emotion lighting up her whole face.

"Where on earth did you find her?"

Amanda quickly told the excited lady about how she'd discovered the missing necklace taped to the bottom of a drawer in the little train depot. The cold wind was whipping around the edge of the porch but Mrs. Welch made no move to invite the chilled couple inside, even though she was only wearing a thin cardigan over her t-shirt and jeans. She kept nodding her head as she listened to Amanda's story, and then asked a couple of questions about who they thought might have hidden Moonlight, her hands still full of her lost treasure.

Amanda was careful to only reply in generalities, knowing that James needed to have the details kept private until the case was solved.

There were tears at the corners of Mrs. Welch's eyes. "I can't thank you enough, Amanda. You don't know what this means to me."

James put up one finger to interrupt the conversation, a hint of humor in his eyes. "I only have one question. Why is the Moonlight Necklace a 'she'?"

Mrs. Welch flexed her lips in the semblance of a smile. "My husband said that years ago it was named after a woman who was nicknamed Moonlight. You don't think anything this beautiful and feminine would be named after a man, do you?"

James shifted a bit, maybe trying to keep warm. "Definitely not," he agreed. "Okay, I have just one more question. I looked through the police report you filed when the necklace first went missing, and it seems like you were never quite sure how it had disappeared. The report said that you remembered putting the necklace in the safe one night and when you checked the safe about a week later it was gone. Is that correct?"

Mrs. Welch pulled her shapeless cardigan around herself more tightly. "It is. I'm absolutely sure that it was put away in that safe and then it just disappeared. There was no evidence of a burglary or anyone tampering with the safe or anything in the house. When I discovered Moonlight was gone I filed the police report right away and started running ads in the paper." She smiled again, still clutching her necklace. "I never expected to see her again in a million years."

James stuck his hands in his deep pockets. "So, you never received an insurance payout for its loss?"

Mrs. Welch's face fell. "No," she said quietly. "I didn't. There wasn't any insurance on it."

"Would you mind me coming in to take a look at the safe?"

Mrs. Welch looked startled at James' request, opening her mouth to respond then clapping it shut. After a second's pause, she said, "I'm so sorry, but I've just had the carpets cleaned and they're still damp. I'm afraid it wouldn't be possible for me to invite visitors inside today."

She nodded at the shivering couple, her thin lips curved up but her voice serious. "Thank you so much for bringing Moonlight back. I'm sorry, but I have to go now."

James stepped toward her, about to ask another question, but Mrs. Welch had already turned and sidestepped through the barely-open doorway, closing it behind her with a loud click.

Amanda glanced at James, who was looking thoughtful. "Okay, that was weird," he finally said.

She knew he was pondering their odd encounter, but after standing on the windswept porch for so long, she had just one thing on her mind.

"Hey, I'm freezing. Last one to the car buys lunch!" she said as she sprinted toward the still-warm SUV, her keys in hand. There was a bark of laughter and she heard the thunder of cowboy boots on the concrete, trying to catch up to her as she ran. They reached the car at the same time, James successfully getting in before she was able to push the button to lock him out.

"You're weird, lady."

She smiled as she turned on the ignition. "You keep saying that, but you also keep asking me out. What does that say about *you*?"

He laughed, but was quiet for a couple of minutes as she drove back toward the main part of town. "You ever heard of anyone shampooing their carpets in the middle of December?"

"In LA maybe, but not around here." Even though the weather was dryer than it had been in weeks, the winter chill was settling on the small town like a blanket. "I'd think she'd want to clean her carpets when the weather's warm, so she could open her windows and let everything dry faster. Even with a good cleaning machine there's still a lot of water left behind."

"Exactly." He leaned back in his seat. "Mrs. Welch really didn't want us in her house, and I'd certainly love to know why."

Chapter 12

There were definitely worse ways to spend a spare few minutes on a cold morning than sitting next to Mrs. Granger and Mrs. Bitterman in Petrie's general store. The old, wooden benches were warm next to the pot-bellied stove, and Amanda welcomed a break in her errands to sit and catch up on the local gossip. Petting Brian Petrie's gray cat, she couldn't help but admire how industrious both of the older ladies were. They were busy knitting while chatting, and Amanda suddenly wished that she hadn't given up when her friend Beth had tried to teach her how to knit a couple of years before.

"I don't know how you can deal with all those guests you have at the Ravenwood Inn," Mrs. Bitterman commented as she expertly looped a bit of yarn around her knitting needle. "It must be difficult with all those strangers coming and going and asking questions about what to do in the area. Don't you get tired of cleaning up after everyone?"

Amanda laughed softly and took one of the frosted cashew cookies that Mrs. Bitterman offered. "Actually, I love it. I can have as many people stay as I want, and if I need a day or two off I just say the Inn's fully booked. Also"— she commented, waving her cookie at the rapt audience in front of her— "so far all my guests have been pretty nice. I've had a couple that started off cranky but even they relaxed enough that they were in a better mood by the end of their stay."

Mrs. Granger nodded, her eyes intent on the half-formed scarf she was knitting. "They were all nice except for that hit man guy. I didn't approve of him at all."

Amanda laughed. "Well, except for him, yes."

"And it must help to have Jennifer Peetman working with you at the Inn, too, doesn't it?"

"She's a sweetheart," Mrs. Bitterman pronounced, setting down her yarn and picking up her mug of hot apple cider.

Amanda opened her mouth to reply but Mrs. Granger cut her off. "Okay," she said, looking over the top of her reading glasses. "Let's get down to brass tacks. What's going on with you and James? He's almost like part of my family, you know, and I'd like to think that you're a nice girl who appreciates a nice boy."

"Well—" Amanda struggled for a response, "— we're dating."

The old lady rolled her eyes and Mrs. Bitterman giggled.

Mrs. Granger got right to the point. "I *know* that. The whole of Ravenwood Cove *knows* that. What I mean is, what are your intentions?"

Amanda couldn't hold back her surprise. "You mean...you mean you want to know if I'm going to make an honest man out of him?"

"Something like that."

"Um..."

Mrs. Granger leaned forward, her knitting forgotten. "Spill it, girlie. What's the scoop with you two?"

Amanda suppressed a grin. "I can tell you one thing."

The old lady's face was expectant. "What?"

"He's an amazing kisser."

She couldn't help but laugh out loud at the look of disgust she got from the old lady, who shook her knitting at Amanda for emphasis. "There are some things I just don't need to know, thank you very much. I prefer to think of him as the sweet boy that I helped raise."

"What did you think I was going to tell you? That I was pregnant with twins?" Amanda leaned over and gave Mrs. Granger a peck on the cheek. "He's a nice guy and I like him. That's it. If anything ever happens that's big news, I promise you'll be the first to know, okay? Just don't hold your breath."

That seemed to satisfy Mrs. Granger and she winked at Amanda. After a few more minutes of chatting, and learning about Grace TwoHorses' new venture selling Kazoodles' toys on a website and that Heinrich's Pizzeria had passed a surprise health inspection with a perfect score of one hundred percent, Amanda gathered her things to go. She was just standing and saying her goodbyes when Solomon Culpepper walked by their cozy little spot. He was carrying a full armload of boxed Christmas lights but he set them down on the top of a nearby oak barrel so he could greet the ladies.

Mrs. Granger kept knitting but crooked a finger at him, pointing toward the boxes. "Looks like you're 'bout ready for Christmas, Solomon. What're you working on today?"

"Just putting some lights up for Jeff at the butcher shop. I guess he didn't think that smoked hams and hanging sausage links were quite festive enough so I'm going to install a new electrical outlet for the front display window." Solomon dug around in the front pocket of his overalls and pulled out a card. He handed it to a surprised Amanda.

"If you ever need any help around the Inn, anything at all, you can call me. I have special winter rates right now, and I could give you a free bid. Roy gets busy sometimes and I could help you, too, ya know."

Amanda was comfortable and happy with her contractor, Roy Greeley. He did good work on time, and he cleaned up his mess when he was done with a project. If he didn't know how to do something he would always tell her, and he did his best to keep costs down.

"Thanks, Solomon. I'll keep you in mind," she said, as she slid the well-worn business card into her purse. She was loyal to Roy, but if there was ever a disaster, it didn't hurt to know a backup handyman.

His pockets stuffed with at least four of Mrs. Bitterman's cashew cookies, Solomon waved a friendly goodbye and headed out the door, squeezing between the displays of artificial Christmas trees. Mrs. Granger had already pronounced the fake trees as 'an abomination" and Amanda secretly agreed.

The moment Solomon was gone, Mrs. Granger felt free to give her opinion.

"He's a nice kid, but he really does need to learn how to dress, and after mending everyone else's fence in town you'd think he'd be able to keep his up a little nicer. I hardly even see him anymore since Bertie left him."

Amanda curbed a smile at Mrs. Granger's comments. To her, anyone under seventy was a kid.

"You know what he needs?" Mrs. Bitterman added, whipping yarn around her clacking needles. "He needs to meet someone. *That's* what he needs."

"Someone who likes cleaning up sawdust and paint on his coveralls," Mrs. Granger added, peering at her knitting as she tried to pick up a dropped stitch. "You know what I heard about Desmond Martin?"

That immediately perked up Amanda's ears. The only news she'd heard about the dead man was from what James had told her and what Lisa had written in the local paper.

Mrs. Granger continued, seeming to have solved her yarn dilemma as she began to knit again. "I heard that Mrs. Mason actually kicked him out of the bakery once, right out onto the sidewalk. Rumor has it that she was yelling at him so hard her face was nearly *purple*. Guess he'd been in there saying he wanted a job and when Mrs. Mason came back with the application form he had his hands on Celia's caboose! Both hands, right behind the counter!"

Mrs. Bitterman looked suitably appalled. "The cheeky little so-and-so."

"Absolutely. He was grabbing her unmentionables and when Mrs. Mason came back into the bakery Celia was so upset she was actually crying. Can you imagine working and having some sicko come in and put his hands on you? Honestly, I don't know what the world's coming to these days," she muttered darkly as she finished off her row of knitting with vigor, as if she was ready to use the needles as weapons on very bad men.

Mrs. Bitterman made sure to stuff Amanda's purse with cookies, just like she'd done with Solomon, and by the time Amanda was at the front counter to pay for the heavy-duty extension cords she'd come in to buy, she was already sure the poor cookies were crumbling at the bottom of her new handbag.

Brian seemed to be in a very festive mood as he rang up her purchases, whistling to himself as he punched the keys on the register.

"Did Mrs. Granger actually call my artificial trees abominations?"

Amanda tried to keep from looking guilty. "I...um...you'd have to ask her."

Brian sighed and smiled a bit. "She does it every year. It's like our holiday tradition. Honestly, I think I'd almost be disappointed if she didn't complain about them."

As Amanda handed him the money she couldn't help but admire a beautiful menorah that had been placed on the shelf behind the register. It was antiqued silver, with intricate carvings and white tapers in each of the eight holders.

Following her gaze, Brian pointed at the menorah. "Stunning, isn't it? It was my mother's."

"So, that probably explains why I never see you working Saturdays." Amanda commented and Brian nodded.

"Yep, and it doesn't hurt that I have a great assistant manager to cover for me. Sally really knows the business."

"Brian, I like Sally, but she forgets my frequent shopper discount sometimes. You need to do something about that."

"I'll make sure she remembers next time, I promise. And Merry Christmas to you."

"And Happy Hanukah, my friend."

Chapter 13

Amanda watched Solomon Culpepper's battered pickup truck park in her circular drive, and suppressed a sigh of frustration. If she'd had her way, she'd have waited until Roy Greeley was back from his Christmas vacation and have him fix the two wooden shutters that had been banging upstairs, but with guests coming and going at all hours at the Inn she needed to be sure everything was in tip top shape. She certainly couldn't have shutters swinging in the wind, disturbing her guests, even if they were located several rooms away from the noise.

She opened the front door and mustered her best smile. "Thanks for coming, Solomon! I really do appreciate it."

His grin was huge, as if he'd won some jackpot. "Oh, I appreciate you calling me, Amanda. I know I'm not your normal fix-it guy, but I want you to know that I give a good job for a good wage." He stepped in the large foyer and looked around appreciatively.

"Wow! I haven't been in this place for years, not since your uncle and aunt owned it. I thought it would be in much worse shape than this, after being abandoned for so long."

Amanda smiled. If there was a way to get in her good graces, it was for someone to compliment her Inn and to recognize the work she'd put into making sure that it was beautiful and loved once again. "It was in pretty rough shape when I got it, but Roy's been able to fix anything I can't." She pointed to the curved staircase. "That's our next project. It's got some damaged areas I'm going to have him repair when he gets back."

Solomon nodded, his smile still in place. "Well, then I can understand why you like to work with him so much. He's a good guy, all right. We go fishing together a couple of times a year, and his sister is friends with my —" Solomon stopped mid-sentence, "—well, I know his sister."

Amanda instantly remembered that Mrs. Granger had told her that Solomon's wife had left him a while ago. Flustered, she was just about to offer him some coffee when Solomon picked up his toolbox, apparently ready to start work. "Just point me to what you need fixed and I'll get you back up and running again."

It didn't take long for Amanda to realize that Solomon was true to his word. He did do a good job, finding the problem with the swinging shutters and figuring out how to fix them. She was a bit nervous when she saw how far he was leaning over the iron railing of the small balcony so he could screw a couple of slotted screws in place to secure everything. It took her a moment to realize that he'd used his belt to secure himself to the railing, but then she knew that even though it looked like dangerous acrobatics, he was being careful not to fall and get hurt.

The main difference between Solomon and Roy was that Solomon was a talker. He gave her a running commentary on what he was doing, how he'd met her uncle at a clam bake the Rotary Club had sponsored, and how he wanted to trade in his truck for a newer model. He had questions about the newspaper article he'd read about the diamond necklace being returned, and told her that he was really happy Mrs. Welch had such good luck that her property had been found. Amanda actually enjoyed sitting on the guest room bed and chatting with him.

After he'd moved to the second bedroom and set his tools down, Amanda was trying to think of topics of conversation. "So, how did it go with your job at Mrs. Sandford's art gallery?"

"Oh, when I fixed the back door? It went fine. She made me come back twice to do it over again but I'm kind of used to that with her, so I always charge her more." Solomon gave Amanda a broad wink and she laughed.

"Sounds fair." She crossed her ankles and swung her legs a bit, relishing the chance to be off her feet. "Solomon, you don't happen to know what sort of business Mrs. Sanford has with Mrs. Welch, do you?" At his startled glance she explained, "I just meant that I saw something of Mrs. Welch's for sale in Mrs. Sanford's gallery."

He straightened up, surprised. "Well, I wouldn't know anything about that. I just work for the ladies, that's all."

Instantly embarrassed for asking such a leading question, Amanda tried to backtrack. "I'm sorry, Solomon. I didn't mean to pry."

The handyman pulled a couple of long screws from his toolbox. "I heard about how you two didn't get along real well when you got to town." He looked at her, waiting to see what she'd say.

Amanda shrugged. "We're just different people, that's all. She's probably the best-heeled lady in town and I think I kind of upset the status quo." She tried to smile but it didn't feel genuine at all.

Solomon nodded. "If I were a single man, I could do worse than to have a rich lady like Hortense Sandford," he teased. "I wouldn't mind being a kept man."

The words were out of Amanda's mouth before she could stop them. "Oh, I thought you were single." Amanda winced, wanting to clap a hand over her mouth. When was she going to be mature enough to not say stupid things?

"Well, technically married," Solomon said as he readied his drill. "Can't afford to track down my ex and get a divorce just yet. Maybe someday." He shrugged. "I know people talk about me and Bertie. There's people in my family that are real mad about the whole thing and I got tired of them talking about me and stuff they didn't know anything about. They didn't know half the details of it, and they blew it up into some big scandal."

He straightened up and looked at Amanda. "Sometimes it isn't drama that ends a marriage. Sometimes people just run out of steam."

"I guess so." Amanda thought back to her relationship with her ex-boyfriend, Ken. They hadn't just run out of stream; they'd gone off the rails.

Solomon stuffed the screws in the front pocket of his overalls. "So, what's new with Desmond Martin? I heard you were doing some investigating for the sheriff's office or something. Spending lots of time talking to the cops, I guess." His voice was serious but Amanda caught the humorous glint in his eye.

"Nothing official."

"You just hang out with the local detective quite a bit, eh?" When Amanda opened her mouth to answer, Solomon kept talking. "Did you know he lived close to where I grew up? Desmond Martin, I mean. He always was a squirrelly guy. Used to fall head over heels for whatever girl would give him the time of day. I think he was engaged about three times when he was still in high school. He was mooning around after my niece for a while until I chased him away."

Amanda watched as he attached his belt to the railing again and leaned out to fix the shutter. Conversation over, she headed downstairs to do the prep work for tomorrow's breakfast. She knew that Solomon had everything well in hand.

Chapter 14

"I think my new bookstore is haunted."

Amanda stopped petting Benny for a moment, stunned. The little dog shifted in her lap, waiting patiently for more attention. "Truman, why would you think that your place is haunted? Everyone loves your bookstore, and I haven't heard a word about anyone thinking there was a ghost in there."

Truman leaned forward in his upholstered chair and tapped one finger against his temple, several silver rings glittering on his fingers. "I'm not crazy, Amanda. Stuff's happening around this place. Supernatural stuff. I can feel it. I'm very sensitive to that sort of energy." One of the bookstore's customers, who had just pulled a large volume out of the Historic Art section, shot Truman a startled glance and quickly moved to a different bookcase. Apparently, their conversation wasn't the sort of talk that set people at ease.

"What sort of supernatural stuff?" Benny nosed Amanda's hand, demanding more attention, and she automatically began to pet him again.

"Things are getting moved, and some things are missing. After I go to sleep, I wake up and I think I hear footsteps but nobody's there." He gave a melodramatic shiver. "It's giving me the creeps. It's not like it's a nice spirit, either. I've gone downstairs in the morning and found a book flung face down on a side table, and the front door's still locked tight as a drum. Something from another dimension is in here, I swear."

Amanda had a flashback to the first time she'd walked into the abandoned Ravenwood Inn. It has been full of cobwebs and memories, and she remembered wondering if a ghost or two was going to waft down the staircase to greet her. Maybe ghosts were real or maybe they weren't, but she wasn't going to mention that.

Amanda loved Benny's Books. It smelled of old paper and fresh coffee, with comfortable chairs and little tables so patrons could sit and look through the books. Truman had made sure to include plenty of used books among the new ones, and the place always seemed to have a steady stream of customers coming and going.

"Truman, I don't think this place is haunted. How could a store that's so warm and fun and popular have ghosts in it? It'd have to be a dead booklover who just wants to browse a bit."

He didn't laugh at her little joke. "I'd think it was a burglar, but there's no other way to get in this side of the building, and there's never any money missing." He got up and automatically started shelving a couple of books that had been left out on side tables, his mind obviously not on what he was doing. "I'd set up security cameras but I've sunk just about every dime I have into the bike store and this place and I can't afford them right now. I keep a baseball bat behind the counter in case of a robbery, but that doesn't help much in a case like this."

"Can you get a friend to stay downstairs one night? Maybe they could see what was going on?"

Truman smiled indulgently. "If I tell them I think the place is haunted, I don't think I'd get many takers. Nobody would want to stay locked inside with a ghost who moves things."

True. Amanda shivered at the thought. She wouldn't want to be the person who stayed overnight. She watched Truman moving from shelf to shelf, carefully arranging the books and greeting an occasional customer. His plaid flannel shirt was unbuttoned and the sleeves rolled up, showing the Ramones t-shirt underneath. For all his courtesy, intelligence, and stylish flair, he didn't seem eager to confront a floating spirit, either.

"What are you going to do about it?"

He paused, book in hand. "I'm not sure yet. Maybe I'll just leave out food and a welcoming note so they leave me alone? Right here "—he slapped a hand on the counter— "I could leave it some angel food cake. That'd suit a ghost." He winked at Amanda, and she laughed.

"How about devil's food? Or maybe it would prefer some alcoholic spirits."

Truman smiled. "You're weird, Amanda."

She grinned back at her friend, noticing that his new haircut included blue tips on the longer hair on the right side, and he was sporting a new earring. "So I've been told. Must mean I'm living in the right town."

Chapter 15

It was a rare day that Amanda got a chance to visit both Meg and Lisa at their workplaces, so when she had a chance to have her morning mocha at Cuppa, and then meet up with Lisa for some much-needed holiday shopping, it made her smile.

The weather had cleared up and the sky was a brilliant, cold blue, and when she stopped by the newspaper office she wasn't surprised to see a pair of kittens rolling around on the floor in a playful wrestling match.

Being careful with the door, she closed it behind her and knelt down, only to become the newest plaything the kittens attacked.

"I see you've met the welcoming committee." Lisa looked over from her desktop and smiled at her friend. "Be careful. They're still so little that sometimes they forget and will nibble a bit."

"I'll watch my fingers. Which ones are these?"

Lisa leaned over and checked. "Moski and Finn. Jasmine's still asleep in the basket. Did you like my article about the Moonlight Necklace?"

"Good stuff," Amanda agreed. "You ready to go?"

"Sure." Amanda gave the kittens one last bit of petting and stood up. "What's on our list today?"

"Well, I need to stop by Mrs. Sandford's and get her approval on the new ad layout, and I was hoping the bookstore might have something about antique motorcycles. You still want to shop at Kazoodles?" Lisa closed her laptop and picked up her gloves. "I didn't know you had kids on your Christmas list."

"Well, I don't, but I thought I'd see what was on sale. I'm trying to put together a toy box for the Inn, so the kids would have something to play with. You really have to stop by the antique store?"

Lisa pulled on her parka and zipped it up. "Is that okay? I know she's not your favorite person in the world but I should be able to be in and out really fast."

Remembering back to how Mrs. Sandford had treated her when she first moved to Ravenwood Cove, Amanda wasn't thrilled at the prospect of walking into her high-end art gallery and antique store. She could still remember how the imperious woman had done her best to shut down the Ravenwood Inn, even if it ruined Amanda's life. She'd learned that in a small town she didn't get the luxury of avoiding someone forever, even if she didn't like that.

Amanda sighed. "That's fine. Maybe I'll do some shopping there."

Lisa scoffed. "Too rich for my blood. Think I'll save my money for lunch."

Standing by the door of Sandford Art Gallery ten minutes later, Amanda was rethinking her decision to go inside. "Maybe I'll just stay on the sidewalk," she said, hunching down into her coat collar to try to stave off the swirling winter wind.

"Nonsense," Lisa said, gently taking her arm. "You can't hide from her forever. You can do this, and I'm right here with you. Come on."

"I really wish you weren't so practical," Amanda muttered as her fearless friend pulled her through the engraved glass door.

The interior was everything Amanda thought it would be. Modern spotlights spilled pools of light on the sumptuous carpet, highlighting antiques so costly and unique that they were displayed as individual works of art. Beautiful furniture was placed strategically around the room, and gleaming glass cases held smaller pieces, including two full lengths of nothing but jewelry. A frosted glass wall at the back separated the office from the showroom floor.

A very pretty blonde woman with flawless makeup walked toward them, her hair gathered into a sculpted ponytail that was meant to look casual and probably had taken an hour to arrange.

"Welcome. My name is Marissa. Is there anything in particular—" she broke off her greeting mid-sentence, apparently recognizing Lisa. "Oh, hello. Mrs. Sanford is in the back. I'll just let her know that you're here." She turned without a word and sauntered gracefully back to the glass wall, speaking quietly at the small window. In less than a minute, Mrs. Sandford emerged from the back room. Amanda felt her spine stiffen.

The ex-mayor had the same regal bearing and frosty expression that she'd had the day Amanda had met her, when Mrs. Sandford had told her that she'd be unable to open the Ravenwood Inn to guests. It had taken every bit of courage and grit Amanda had to dig in and fight for the right to have a business in Ravenwood Cove, and she'd been rewarded with good friends and a new hometown that she'd grown to love. Amanda had remembered that James had said Mrs. Sandford hadn't had as easy a life as she pretended, and that had given Amanda the ability to be a bit sympathetic to the older lady, but it was still difficult to even be around her.

Seeing Amanda standing with Lisa, Mrs. Sandford seemed to pause mid-stride, before turning slightly away.

"I take it you have the ad copy we discussed?" she asked, her voice cool as she ignored Amanda.

"Of course," Lisa replied, placing a set of printouts on the nearby glass counter.

Cut out of the conversation, Amanda walked over to the nearby jewelry counter. She'd been wanting to get something for her friend Beth, who'd helped her move from LA to Ravenwood Cove, and looking over the collection, she could tell that almost everything in the case was over her gift budget.

Still, it was fun to look. She could hear that Lisa and Mrs. Sanford seemed to be wrapping up their business discussion and by the time Lisa walked over to join her she'd found several necklaces that she particularly liked.

"Did she like your design?" Amanda asked, not moving her head as she looked at the jewelry.

She could feel the shrug Lisa gave. "She did what she always does. Critiques it, corrects it, and asks me when I can make her changes. Find anything you want?"

"Too much, I'm afraid, but I'd have to win the lottery before I could buy them." She pointed a couple pieces out to Lisa, when suddenly she realized that her friend has fixated on a particular necklace. It was two loops of flawless white pearls and a stunning gold dragon pendant with bright emeralds set as the eyes.

"I know that piece." Lisa's voice was deadly serious and Amanda turned to look at her.

"You've seen it before?"

"Yes. Let's go." Lisa darted a glance toward the back of the store, while she gave Amanda a gentle push toward the doorway.

Amanda was puzzled but played along, turning to look at Lisa the moment they were outside and walking toward Petrie's.

"What was all that about?"

Lisa gripped her upper arm and pulled her into the nearby alleyway, out of the wind. Making sure no one was around, she let go of Amanda's arm and started to explain.

"Okay, so you know that pearl necklace that we were looking at? Well, it actually belongs to Mrs. Welch, but I have no idea what it's doing for sale in Mrs. Sandford's store. She used to wear that necklace all the time when they were out on the town, like to a play or concert or something. I can't remember a time when she was dressing up when she wasn't wearing those pearls."

Amanda was surprised. "I thought she wore her diamond necklace."

Her friend shook her head. "No, I never saw her wear that. Just heard about it several times. Mr. Welch used to brag about how much money he was making in his different business ventures, and he sure liked showing off how well they were doing. He used to point out that necklace, saying that a true lady always wore good pearls." She bit her lip, deep in thought. "Mrs. Welch wouldn't give up that necklace unless she really needed to sell it."

Amanda flashed back to when she'd been at Mrs. Welch's house, and the odd encounter on the unmaintained front porch. "Maybe she's in financial trouble."

Lisa looked at her and screwed up her mouth. "Maybe Mr. Welch wasn't quite as flush as he said he was. Either that, or something's happened. Whichever it is, it would explain why she paid for the last newspaper ad she bought with two rolls of quarters, and why she was desperate to get the necklace back."

"She wouldn't let us in her house."

"What?" Lisa asked, focusing again on Amanda.

"She kept us out on the front porch, shivering, and said she was having her carpets shampooed so we couldn't come in." Amanda frowned. "What's Mrs. Sandford's first name again?"

"Hortense."

Amanda nodded. "When Mrs. Welch came out of her house she said she thought that we were Hortense, coming back. That means Mrs. Sandford was in the house." She thought for a moment. "Sounds like Mrs. Welch is keeping secrets."

They stood in the cold, both considering the possibilities.

Amanda finally made a decision. "Well, it's nothing that we can fix standing here. Let's go into Petrie's and warm up. Mrs. Granger said that they'd just started selling bunches of fresh mistletoe, cut off Mrs. Bitterman's big oak trees. I think I'll surprise Meg and put a big ball of mistletoe up inside the front door of Cuppa for her."

Lisa laughed. "You're incorrigible," she said, but walked into the general store with Amanda, ready to buy mistletoe.

Chapter 16

It had been a long day, and Amanda was happy to be driving home from the food bank.

Earlier in the afternoon, she'd picked up the donated food from the Grange hall and packed her car full of dozens of boxes and bags of groceries. It was about a twenty-minute drive to the nearby food bank in Morganville, and she didn't mind. It was a beautifully-clear, cold day, but when she arrived at the small warehouse she'd discovered that there was no one to help her unload. A balding man with a clipboard and a harried expression was talking animatedly with a thick-set truck driver about where to offload his delivery. When Amanda asked where he wanted her items to go, he pointed to a spot where she could set the bags and boxes on the dock but offered her no assistance. Looking around, there didn't seem to be anyone else who worked there, so she had gamely unpacked the entire car. Bags weren't difficult to set on the dock, but the full cases of canned goods were heavy and unwieldy, making it difficult to heft them into place. It was amazing how many pounds of food she'd been able to cram into her SUV, but she hadn't considered the possibility of getting her workout just by moving groceries.

Her muscles were aching a bit as she drove back, but she was humming happily, thinking of the families who would soon have some extra Christmas cheer in their kitchens. She'd been kind of insulated from hunger when she lived in LA, not paying much attention to the many homeless and struggling people who were around her, but Ravenwood Cove was different. It was so small that the person facing hunger was possibly a neighbor or a coworker, and it felt good to giving something back to the community.

Maybe she needed to start thinking more about the needy people she couldn't see.

The country road wound through some hills that she hadn't explored before, and as she got closer to town, she realized that she'd be driving very close to the mysterious Mrs. Welch's home.

Before she knew it, she'd swung her car right, around the corner and down the treed avenue. There were several large, handsome houses on the block, with only Mrs. Welch's home not having some sort of Christmas lights or yard decorations for the season. Other yards had colored lights wrapped around shrubs and big trees, with some people lining their front porch or windows with little white lights, but Mrs. Welch's seemed dark and silent.

Slowing a bit, she peered at the once-proud home, thinking about the necklace for sale at Mrs. Sandford's shop, and how Mrs. Welch had been so careful not to let her and James into her house. She glanced around, making sure no one was peering at her car moving slowly through the neighborhood, when she saw a bit of furtive movement at the edge of Mrs. Welch's yard. There was a rustling of the rhododendron bushes, and she caught a glimpse of a tall shadow moving behind them, toward the back yard.

All of Amanda's warning flags went off. The secretive figure sure didn't move like Mrs. Welch would have, and it seemed that whoever it was meant to stay as hidden as possible. There was no sign of Solomon's handyman truck or any other vehicle, and whoever it was definitely didn't look like they belonged on that side yard.

Driving two doors down from Mrs. Welch's, Amanda pulled her car next to the curbed sidewalk, and turned it off. She got out and shut the door behind her as quietly as she could. She swiveled her head around, looking for anyone else who might be in the area but didn't see anyone, even at the neighboring windows. The late afternoon light was fading a bit, but she knew that if she could see someone prowling around the dark house, someone else would be able to see her, too.

After a bit of quick thinking, Amanda decided that walking down the public sidewalk would be infinitely safer than trying to sneak around after a mysterious stranger. Trying to muster an air of confidence, she squared her shoulders and wrapped her scarf more tightly around her neck, heading toward Mrs. Welch's house like she had every reason in the world to be strolling down that sidewalk.

Trying to act casual, she glanced around and finally caught sight of the lurking person again, circling around the back porch and walking out toward the sidewalk from the other side yard.

It was a man, tall, carrying a cane or something in his hands. Amanda ducked her head down as if studying the ground as she continued walking past Mrs. Welch's imposing house. The man was hesitating near the sidewalk, and Amanda could tell the moment he caught sight of her because he pivoted and walked very quickly away from her. Without glancing back, he suddenly picked up speed and started to sprint away, ducking down a side street. By the time Amanda was close enough to see around the corner the mysterious man was gone, as if he'd never been there.

Amanda walked quickly back to her car, her thoughts whirling with the strange encounter. Whatever the lurking man had wanted, whatever he was searching for, Amanda now knew one thing about him.

Mrs. Welch's odd visitor had been carrying a very familiar-looking metal detector.

Chapter 17

"Celia, you're a lifesaver."

The cheerful girl laughed at Amanda's compliment. "It sounded like you needed them right away and I don't live too far from here. It's no problem at all."

Amanda opened the large box of freshly-baked pastries and took a deep, satisfying whiff. "I know the bakery usually doesn't do deliveries, but I've been so crazy busy with guests that I forgot to get the cinnamon rolls at Cuppa for tomorrow's breakfast. They were already closed by the time I called." She looked up, startled, to see Celia looking back at her. A smile played around the baker's lips.

"It's okay for you to talk about Cuppa. I know you're friends with Meg, and we don't actually compete that much with each other. We don't serve coffee."

You may not compete with Cuppa, but their cinnamon rolls still beat yours, hands down, Amanda thought as she thanked Celia again for the pastries.

She could hear a lot of laughing and running upstairs, with occasional thumps and raised voices. Celia glanced toward the curved staircase.

"How many guests do you have here today? Sounds like a herd of elephants."

Amanda grinned. "Nope, just a pair of eight-year-old twins, an angsty thirteen-year-old girl, and a set of really tired parents. That's the twins you're hearing. I gave them some Nerf guns and let them have a shootout in the hallway."

Celia raised her eyebrows. "Do you usually let your guests do that?"

"Not usually, but they're the only guests I have right now, and there's nothing breakable in the hallway. It seemed like a way to get some of that energy used up." Amanda laughed. "I think the parents actually went to take a nap while their kids are having a shootout. Must be nice to be able to sleep through anything."

"I'm more of an insomniac myself." Celia sat down on the nearby bar stool and leaned her elbows on the marble top of the kitchen island. "So, I heard you're probably in the know about what's going on with the Desmond Martin investigation. Can I ask you about it or will it make you uncomfortable?"

"No, it's okay," Amanda said as she stashed the bakery box in the large pantry. "I just don't know everything, that's all. There seem to be more questions about him than answers." She rummaged around in the fridge for a minute, pulling out a bowl of chilled fruit. Gathering up a cutting board and a sharp knife, she set them on the island and went to wash her hands at the sink.

"Ask away," she said, turning off the running water.

"Well, they said he was shot. Do they have any leads about that?"

Amanda dried her hands on a clean towel and stood across from Celia, reaching underneath the island to get a large pottery bowl. Tomorrow's breakfast would include a fruit salad and some crispy bacon, and she had time to get the fruit cut up ahead of time.

"Not that they're telling me about," she said as she expertly peeled one of the cold oranges. "Mrs. Mason told me you met Desmond Martin at the bakery one day."

Celia shuddered. "Yes, meeting him once was plenty for me. What a creep!"

"I heard he was harassing you." Amanda didn't add that he'd been discovered pawing Celia's backside before Mrs. Mason had thrown him out of the bakery in a fit of protective rage.

"It was horrible. I've never had anyone...bother me like that. So humiliating!" Amanda could see the tears gathering in the corners of the younger woman's eyes, and stopped what she was doing.

"I'm sorry, Celia. I didn't mean to upset you."

Celia's chin was quivering with emotion. "Thank goodness Mrs. Mason walked in on him right then. Who knows what else he would've tried, with his criminal past and all."

"I heard he asked Mrs. Mason for a job that day."

Celia set her hands on the smooth marble. "Yes, he did. He didn't have any experience but she was still going to interview him. She's got a soft spot for people who need a job and are willing to learn."

Amanda nodded in silent agreement. Celia cleared her throat and mustered a smile. "Mrs. Mason's been almost like a mother to me, you know. I got really lucky that she hired me at all. My last job in Kansas was as a dishwasher, and she's teaching me so much about business and the bakery."

Amanda dumped the chopped orange in the bowl. "Oh, I thought Mrs. Mason said you were from Oklahoma."

Celia laughed and shook her head. "She's a sweetie, but she's not much on geography. I think she thinks that any state in the middle of America is Oklahoma. I'm a fighting Jayhawk, born and bred. I only came out here because my mom passed away and I have family in Oregon, so I thought it would be a good place to make a new start." She brightened up. "I've got my own apartment here, you know. It's the first time I haven't had to have a roommate or been with my Mom."

Peeling a papaya, Amanda smiled. "Sounds like a big step for you. Congratulations!" She thought back to the loss of her own mother and felt a pang of sympathy for the soft-spoken girl sitting across from her. "Must be tough to start in a new town. I did it here at Ravenwood Cove, too. Everyone's lived here so long that I still feel like a newcomer, even though most people are really friendly."

Celia seemed to agree. "It's not easy, making a new life, is it? I guess some people grow up and have a great life automatically, and some of us have to grab it with both hands and hang on." She sighed and picked up her purse.

"Some of us have to do whatever we can to make our own happiness."

Chapter 18

The text was short and sweet.

IF YOU'LL STAY WITH ME IN THE BOOKSTORE FOR A COUPLE OF HOURS PAST DARK TONIGHT MAYBE WE CAN SEE THE GHOST.

There was a pause of less than a minute before Truman's follow-up text arrived.

I'LL BE THE ONE WITH THE HOLY WATER. :D THANKS

Amanda wasn't exactly thrilled. *That's what I get for telling him that the last two guests for the day had left and there weren't any expected at the Inn until the next afternoon,* she thought darkly as she packed a quilt in her car and glumly drove to Benny's Bookstore.

The antique streetlights were already flickering on in the small downtown of Ravenwood Cove, casting a soft, warm light on the wide sidewalks. Driving by the town square, she could see that whoever was in charge of putting the many strings of white fairy lights up in the trees and around shop awnings and doorways had done an amazing job. Rumor was that the Hortman brothers had been offered the contract by the town council, under the firm provision that they were only to work until noon every day, so there wouldn't be any chance of them drinking and falling off a ladder while on the job. Whether that was true or not, Ravenwood Cove had never looked so festive. The town council had gone door to door, talking to all the shop owners and encouraging them to put their best decorating foot forward, and it had definitely made a difference.

Truman and Benny were waiting when Amanda arrived. She parked at the curb and pulled the fluffy blanket out of the passenger side, all ready for curling up on one of Truman's secondhand sofas and doing some reading. She knew he'd invited her so they could investigate the ghostly occurrences in the shop, but she was more interested in something hot to drink and a bit of reading time with a good book and her new friend.

After a welcoming hug and some chit chat, Amanda settled on a sofa and Benny hopped up in her lap the moment she sat down. Truman flipped over the CLOSED sign and turned off the main lights. He switched on a small lamp on the table next to Amanda and settled into the overstuffed chair close by, pulling out a computer tablet. Peeking at his screen, Amanda watched him flip to a reading app and open up an e-book.

"I'm telling your customers that you don't read your own books," she teased, watching Truman pop his head up in surprise. "You got something against paperbacks?"

He grinned. "My reading tastes are kinda eclectic sometimes, and besides, it's easier to pack a whole library in this thing than it would be to fit the books in my apartment. Now, what's it going to take to buy your silence? Coffee?"

Amanda shook her head. "Cocoa. I'm a woman of discriminating tastes," she said, flipping a page in her book.

Within minutes Truman had brought her preferred bribe, a big mug of cocoa, and they both settled in to read, a companionable silence between them. Benny was content to snuggle on Amanda's lap, finally falling to sleep and occasionally twitching as he dreamed whatever small dogs dream.

The quiet bookstore and the dark room was relaxing, and Amanda had to catch herself from nodding off a couple of times. The warm dog and the calm atmosphere was making her sleepy. Glancing at Truman, she could see he was intent on whatever was on his screen, his eyes flying across the page.

It had been almost an hour of near-silence when the first manifestation of the ghost occurred.

Amanda could hear a slight shuffling, but because of the tall, full bookcases around her she couldn't quite tell which direction it was coming from. Glancing at Truman, she saw him quickly shut his tablet, dousing its light. Amanda reached over and silently turned off the little desk lamp, her eyes wide as she tried to quickly adjust to the new dimness. The only light was coming in from the faint white lights out on the square, and it took her a moment to be able to see again.

There was a long pause. Maybe it was ten minutes, maybe ten heartbeats; Amanda couldn't tell, but at last she heard the faint shuffling again, sounding like it was coming from a space above and behind her. Fumbling for Truman's hand, she was glad to grab on and grateful for the warm squeeze he gave her in return. They waited in silence, not moving, not breathing.

There was the shuffling sound again, and a bit of creaking.

Above them now, and coming closer toward them.

Amanda felt Truman grip her hand more tightly, and suddenly a small chunk of something fell on Amanda's hair.

She squeaked in terror, jumping to her feet and frantically trying to brush the unseen thing off her head, picturing huge spiders and ghostly fingers. Truman quickly clicked on the desk lamp and leaped up, ready to help her. When Amanda looked down, she could see something small lying on the well-worn plank floor.

Plaster. It was a bit of broken plaster that hadn't been there before.

Clutching Truman's arm, she looked up and pointed at the ceiling. There was a small, fresh crack in the ancient plaster above them. The room was suddenly silent and Amanda turned to Truman, her eyes wide.

"You don't have ghosts. You have guests," she mouthed quietly, and she could see the shock in his eyes. Whatever he'd expected, it didn't seem to include the thought that people might be upstairs in his unused garret.

"Should I call the emergency number?" he asked breathlessly, and she nodded.

"Yes, *you* call 'em. I think I've used up my quota with 911 this year."

Chapter 19

Within minutes, two cars full of Ravenwood Cove's entire police force had squealed to a stop in front of Benny's Bookstore. Amanda met them outside and quickly explained the situation, and cautioned them that Truman was still inside, muttering angry oaths at his ceiling and carrying a full-sized baseball bat.

The police were focused and thorough, but after an extensive search of the entire bookstore they found no evidence of anyone living there, except for Truman in the apartment next door. Checking the outside of the building, the only possible way in and out of the attic space was a tiny set of louvered vents at each end of the building, with metal screening over it. The vents were too small to let anyone crawl inside. The police officers were polite but seemed skeptical about someone being upstairs until Amanda pointed out the piece of plaster, freshly broken from the crack in the ceiling.

George Ortiz, the police chief, instructed his crew to check over every bit of wall and ceiling they could, looking for any sort of opening that might be hidden. He told them to check for drafts coming through the decorative moulding around doors, places that looked more worn than something around them, or anything else that might seem unusual.

Amanda watched the whole thing, wishing that James was in town so he could be part of the investigation. She knew it was a local matter that George and his team of officers could handle perfectly well, but she'd still feel more comfortable having James nearby to oversee the situation.

It took almost half an hour, but a triumphant yelp from the back office quickly brought a rush of officers to see what had been discovered. Years ago, someone must've decided that a dropped ceiling would make the unheated office warmer, but when the rookie officer, Rollins, had taken a closer look at the seemingly-nailed on panels, he discovered that one was loose. A quick inspection revealed a square door in the ceiling that would almost certainly open into the attic space.

George had a quick consultation with another officer and took Truman and Amanda aside, his face serious.

"We're going to ask whoever is up there to come out. It's safest for everyone if we don't have to go up and try to corner them."

Amanda gulped. "What if they don't come out? I mean, what do you do?"

"We tell them we're sending in the dog."

"Benny?" Truman squeaked, putting his hand down to pet his little friend.

"No, not Benny," George answered, obviously trying to keep a straight face. "We tell them we have a K-9 unit with a German Shepherd and we're sure they don't want to get bitten. That usually does the trick."

Amanda was puzzled. "Does Ravenwood Cove have a K-9 unit? I don't remember ever – "

George interrupted her. "We don't. Our town is too small to afford or need one, but whoever is upstairs might not know that, right?"

Truman looked relieved. "I guess that makes sense." He picked up Benny and patted him absently. "What do you want us to do?"

"I'd appreciate it if you go outside and just wait. If anything happens we want to make sure that you're out of the line of fire."

With that happy thought in mind, Amanda found herself outside on the sidewalk, standing next to Truman and Benny, waiting. The shop's front door was left open but they couldn't hear much. After a minute or so there was a lot of angry yelling and the loud sound of scuffling, punctuated by a high scream. Truman grabbed Amanda's hand and pulled her a bit farther away as the mayhem inside continued, then suddenly stopped.

Leaning over to peer inside, Amanda could just make out that there was someone lying face down on the floor, with a police officer kneeling on his back and methodically putting him in handcuffs. Two other officers stood by with their guns drawn, pointing them at the suspect, who seemed to have given up. He was lying quietly until the cop on his back moved to stand and pulled the suspect up with him. Speaking calmly to him as he advised the man of his rights, the officer marched him toward one of the nearby sofas and instructed him to sit down.

Officer Rollins motioned for Amanda and Truman to come inside. "We've already cleared the upstairs. This is the only guy."

Just as she walked through the door, Amanda recognized the man's face. She'd seen that face before.

The face of the stranger with a metal detector, killing time in the local restaurants and coffeeshop, and snooping around Mrs. Welch's house.

Truman settled into a nearby chair, staring at the cowed man as if he were truly seeing a ghost. His voice was nearly a whisper. "Who are you and why are you in my bookstore?"

The unshaven man looked up, regret in his eyes. "My name is Henry Crabbe. I'm a numismatist."

"A what?"

"A numismatist. Someone who collects old and valuable coins. Look, I'm really sorry about staying in your attic. I'll repair any damage I've done, I swear. Please don't let them arrest me."

Two of the police officers trickled out, back to their normal patrols since the excitement at the bookstore had died down, but two remained, including George, listening to Henry Crabbe talk.

"I'm sorry about sleeping upstairs. I just needed a safe and dry place to stay while I was here in town. I never meant to scare anyone."

Amanda sat next to Truman. "You didn't answer his question. Why are you here?"

The man turned his sorrowful eyes toward Amanda, and she had the sudden impression she was looking at a sad beagle with droopy ears and a mournful face.

"I just came to get what's owed to me, that's all. I never meant any harm. If he'd just given the money he owed me I wouldn't have had to spend my last dime coming here and trying to find it on my own." He looked at Truman. "By the way, you really should get an alarm system installed here. That back door in the alley was incredibly easy to jimmy open."

Amanda could see that Truman was trying to control his temper. "What are you talking about? Who owed you money?"

Henry blinked at him. "Mr. Welch, of course. Took delivery of some of my best gold coins, saying it was for his collection, and then I found out the money order was no good. It was fake. When I tried to contact him I never heard a word back, even after sending certified letters. His phone number was disconnected. After almost a year I was out of money and at my wit's end, so I decided to confront him in person." He turned to the listening officers. "I wasn't gonna hurt him, honest. I just wanted him to give back my coins and then I would've been on my way, but I didn't know he had died, you see? I had no idea that he'd passed away, and when I saw his widow outside her house one day I talked to her about the whole thing."

Henry looked down and shifted his hands behind him. "Can someone loosen up these cuffs a bit? They're really starting to dig into my wrists."

George Ortiz ignored him. "You talked to Mrs. Welch about the coins? What happened?"

"She said she didn't know a thing about it, and when I tried to talk about it she ran inside and locked the door. Well, I thought her behavior seemed very suspicious, so I kept an eye on the house, you see? Even if Mr. Welch was dead, he hadn't taken my coins to whatever afterlife he wound up going to. I figured that maybe his wife would still have them around, maybe hidden. The problem was, I didn't have a place to stay, and I needed to be in the area in case something turned up." He looked down, visibly upset. "I guess he'd done this sort of thing before, bought coins and then passed bad checks to pay for them. I didn't find out about it until it was too late. Now I'm sitting here in handcuffs and he's dead and I go to jail. End of story."

George's voice was stern. "Were you trying to get the necklace? Was that why you stayed in town?"

"You mean the diamond necklace they talked about in the paper?"

At the police chief's answering nod, Henry Crabbe shook his head adamantly. "I don't know anything about that necklace, I swear! I only read about it two days ago, and I was in Indiana until last Wednesday. Ask Truman! He can tell you that I was only here for less than a week!" He was practically stammering as he tried to explain himself. "I'm only here for what's owed me, and that's the coins."

Amanda could hear the panic in his voice. "Is that why I saw you outside Mrs. Welch's house? You looked like you were searching for something."

Henry looked almost embarrassed. "I figured that if he hadn't gotten rid of the coins and if his wife didn't know about them, maybe he hid them somewhere, or buried them. I know it sounds silly, but I was grasping at straws." He turned to Truman. "I'm real sorry about breaking into your place. I just needed a place out of the weather and I could tell you weren't using it." He looked a bit embarrassed. "Oh, and I'm sorry about eating your tuna sandwich, too. You left it in the little fridge in the office and I didn't think you'd miss it."

Truman's face relaxed into a slow smile. "I'd wondered what happened to that sandwich."

"It was tasty. Thanks."

Looking at Truman's suddenly relaxed posture, Amanda knew that unless there was something truly horrible on Henry Crabbe's record, her soft-hearted friend Truman wouldn't be pressing charges.

After a bit of discussion, the officers escorted Henry Crabbe to the waiting patrol car and carefully put him the back seat, slamming the door behind him. Apparently, they weren't done questioning him about any possible involvement he might have with the necklace or Desmond Martin. Amanda and Truman stood on the sidewalk and watched the car pull away, wondering what Henry Crabbe's fate would be.

"Well, so much for my ghost," Truman commented.

"Told you it wasn't a ghost," Amanda replied, going back inside for her purse.

"Uh-huh. Is that why you screamed when that bit of plaster dropped on your head?"

Amanda tried not to laugh. "It startled me, that's all. I'm heading home to get some sleep."

Driving back to the Inn, she mulled over the night's adventure, thinking back on what Henry Crabbe had said. Some questions had been answered, but he'd actually brought up some new ones. Why had Mr. Welch been passing bad checks? She'd never heard that he was a thief or criminal, or that he'd had any money troubles. All she'd been told was that he was a successful businessman who tended to keep his personal life quiet. He wasn't active in any social clubs or known for having many friends. She thought back to her one encounter with his widow, when Mrs. Welch was so happy to get the necklace back but wouldn't let her and James inside her house.

Definitely something weird there.

Curiouser and curiouser.

Chapter 20

"Mrs. Granger, I'm not giving you any more tape."

The old lady huffed in frustration at Amanda's statement. "I can't help it that I'm not some super-duper wrapping expert. Some of us need more tape than others to get the job done, that's all. Why should I be penalized for making sure the presents I'm wrapping are sealed properly?" She thumped her hand on the Ravenwood Inn's long harvest table for emphasis, trying to ignore the extra bits of tape still stuck to her fingers.

Meg rolled her eyes and peeled a foot-long strip of scotch tape off her grandmother's sleeve. "I think what Amanda meant, Gram, was that she'd be happy to help you with the tape. If we keep up at this rate, the kids' presents won't be wrapped until New Year's Eve, that's all. Pastor Fox said there were forty-two gifts that needed to be wrapped by four o'clock, and we're falling behind. He won't be able to take them over to Likely in time to give out to the children if we don't get these finished."

Amanda picked out a boxed Barbie doll and grabbed a roll of colorful red and gold foil paper. She didn't like putting a damper on Mrs. Granger's enthusiasm to help get toys to kids who otherwise wouldn't have a Christmas present, but the packages were starting to look more and more like they'd been wrapped by someone who'd had a few too many drinks.

"How about we put you in charge of bows?" she offered.

That didn't placate the old lady one bit. "Bows are for losers," she said darkly, as she crossed her arms across her chest in disgust. "I can handle tape."

Glancing over Mrs. Granger's head, Amanda telegraphed a silent plea for Meg to somehow change the subject.

Meg nodded, understanding. "Gram, did you hear about the guy they found who was staying in Truman's attic? Guess he'd been there for a couple of weeks."

Mrs. Granger looked at her like she was an idiot. "Yes, dear, of course I heard about that. Read it in the Tide the day after it happened. I think he's awfully lucky that Truman isn't pressing charges. I'd have had his butt in a sling if he was staying in my attic, eating *my* tuna sandwiches."

Amanda tried not to laugh at the thought of the elderly Mrs. Granger taking down some imaginary fiend who would dare stay in her attic and snoop through her fridge.

She cut a length of paper and carefully pulled it around the doll's box. "I guess they'd been worried he was somehow tied to the Desmond Martin case, but his story checked out. The cops confirmed that he was in Indiana during the time when Martin was murdered, so he's off the hook."

"Well, lucky him," Mrs. Granger said, still crabby.

Meg ignored her grandmother. "I hear Truman's letting him stay in the attic over the bookstore, rent-free. Awfully nice of him. Oh, and on another subject —" she turned to Amanda and shook a pair of closed scissors at her, "—someone came into Cuppa and hung a huge bundle of mistletoe over the doorway. You wouldn't happen to know anything about it, would you?"

It was impossible for Amanda to keep a straight face. "I plead the Fifth."

"I KNEW IT." Meg tried her best to look hurt. "You didn't need to do that, Amanda. It's not like I can't get someone to kiss me without having to resort to mistletoe. I can find my own guys, you know."

Amanda got up and hugged her friend around the shoulders. "It wasn't a statement about you not having a guy right now, sweetie. Lisa and I just thought that it would be a nice addition to the coffeeshop. That's all."

Mrs. Granger nodded, apparently agreeing. "You're a sweet young woman and any man would be lucky to be with you. That being said—" she added, looking over her glasses, "—those eggs of yours aren't getting any fresher at your age, young lady."

"Gram, that's horrible!" Meg's mouth was open in mock offense. She was far too used to her grandmother's eccentricities to be truly shocked by her speaking her mind.

Mrs. Granger put an open hand on her chest. "Horrible? ME? Honey, you know I love you and I always want what's best for you. I'm just saying that you may have to step things up a bit so you don't hit your expiration date, if you know what I mean."

Definitely time to change the subject, Amanda thought, watching the two women frown at each other, the lines in their faces definitely showing a family resemblance.

"So, Mrs. Granger, is it all right if I ask you a few questions about the Welches? I mean, there seems to be some confusion about what type of business Mr. Welch was actually in."

The old lady snorted, her face hardening. "What business *wasn't* he in? Anything that some fool was selling to other fools as a get-rich-quick scheme was exactly the sort of business Mr. Welch liked." She shook the huge red bow in her hand for emphasis, as if she was shaking Mr. Welch himself. "That man lost more money than most people see in a lifetime. Heck, in a dozen lifetimes. He was always moving on to the next new thing and his poor wife was just along for the ride. In the twenty plus years they lived here, he never had a steady job at all. Natural wheeler-dealer."

This was news to Amanda. "What happened when he died? Did he leave anything behind?"

Mrs. Granger shook her head. "I think his widow was lucky to have a roof over her head after he was gone. If he'd lived long enough, he'd probably have lost that, too."

Meg pulled off a large strip of tape and eyeballed the wrapping paper she'd cut, finally deciding that it would just fit the boxed dump truck. "Did they have any kids?"

"Well,"—Mrs. Granger's voice dropped to a near-whisper—"rumor has it that he'd been married before and left his wife and kids somewhere else. Just took 'em home to her mama and dumped them there, then moved out to Ravenwood with a brand-new bride. Of course"— she added innocently, leaning back in her chair— "that all might just be gossip, but I wouldn't know about that."

"Kind of personal, talking about people like that, isn't it?" Amanda asked. She didn't want to sound too judgmental, but sometimes the old lady got a bit too close to gossiping when she talked.

Mrs. Granger looked her in the eye and set down her newly-wrapped package. "It's all public knowledge." She dug another bow out of a nearby plastic bag, then brightened up as if she'd remembered something. "Did you know that I set up a betting pool with the ladies in the historical society? We're trying to figure out who the murderer is."

Meg had been taking a drink of her coffee and her grandmother's bizarre announcement made her choke a bit. "A betting pool? On murder? Gram! That's just sick."

"What?" The old lady managed to look both innocent and surprised at the same time. "It's just a bit of harmless fun. It's not like we killed Desmond Martin ourselves." She grinned. "Besides, the winner gets over a hundred bucks, and that's not chicken feed."

Amanda tried not to laugh. "And you're planning on winning this, I take it?"

"Darn tootin'."

Meg was obviously mulling it over. "Who's the top pick? I mean, who's the odds on favorite?" She waved her hand, as if dismissing a bad thought. "It's not that I still don't think it's a bit morbid. It's just that I'm *interested*, that's all."

"Well, there are several suspects. My money was on Henry Crabbe, but now that he's got an alibi, I'm going to have to change my bet."

Amanda got up and brought a large cardboard box over to the kitchen table so she could put the wrapped presents all together. "Well, we know there's something weird going on with Mrs. Welch. Is she in your betting pool? She's definitely keeping secrets."

Mrs. Granger instantly perked up. "What kind of secrets?"

Amanda knew better than to fall for the innocent look of her ninety-year-old friend. "Nothing to worry about," she said. As crass as a murder betting pool was, giving details of Mrs. Welch's jewelry being up for sale seemed even worse.

Maybe Desmond Martin was bribing her to get Moonlight back, she thought, trying to ignore Mrs. Granger's determined stare. *Maybe she killed him and then found out he didn't have the necklace with him.*

"I think I'm going to put my money on Mrs. Mason," Mrs. Granger said as she sat back in her chair, all pretense of wrapping packages for needy families completely gone. "She's probably a long shot, but I know she couldn't stand that guy, and right now she's the only one we know that was yelling at him publicly."

Meg shook her head. "My money would be on some transient coming through here and killing Desmond Martin for his wallet. You know, they never found that on him, and I hate the thought that someone from Ravenwood Cove might be the killer." She paused, her face sad. "I like the people here. Well, most of them."

Mrs. Granger grinned. "If you want a real long shot, you should bet on Truman. Last I heard he was running at a hundred-to-one."

Setting her tube of wrapping paper down in frustration, Amanda tried to keep her voice even. "Ladies, we need to think about what we're doing. Here we are again, talking about other people."

Mrs. Granger sighed and glanced at her granddaughter. "Beats talking about the expiration date on eggs."

Chapter 21

"There's no way you're gonna get that through the door."

She could barely hear James, and couldn't see him at all, he was so engulfed by the branches of the huge fir tree wedged in the Ravenwood Inn's front doorframe. There was a bit of movement as he readjusted something to try a different angle of approach.

"It'll fit. Give me a minute…"

"I thought George was coming over to help."

Amanda heard a muffled comment, then he replied. "He had to fill in at the Rotary Club meeting. Guess the normal chairman was sick."

"Want a hand with that?" She was pretty sure she knew what his answer was going to be.

"Nope, I got it." From the muttering and the several minutes when the tree hadn't moved any further, Amanda was suspicious that he didn't, but she stepped back and crossed her arms, ignoring the cold air streaming in through the open door and patiently waiting.

A bit of mumbling, a sharp exclamation, and the huge evergreen was finally shoved inside, the branches bouncing into place once they were free of the doorjamb. James popped his head out from the branches by the base, his baseball cap gone and his hair rakishly tousled. Giving her a grin, he said, "Okay, now

I can use some help. Can you grab the top and we'll wrestle it into the stand?"

It was another ten minutes before the massive tree, cut fresh from James' family ranch, was set upright and properly secured in the massive stand by the front parlor window. Oscar had eyed the goings-on with a critical eye, but stayed curled up on the upholstered chair closest to the brick fireplace. His tail twitched from time to time when it seemed that the humans couldn't figure out if the tree was straight or if the stand was in the right spot. Silly humans.

At last the tree was secure and Amanda and James stepped back to survey their accomplishment. It was a beauty, towering at least ten feet tall and filling the Inn with the clean scent of freshly-cut greenery.

"You said you wanted a big one," James said, gesturing at the huge tree. "Should be dry enough by now to decorate. I kept it in that big bucket on the porch, so most of the rain should be off it."

"Well, you did take me at my word. Big it is." Amanda pushed aside a couple of the branches, peering toward the trunk. "Just promise me that nothing's living in there, okay? I don't think I could take finding a squirrel or some critter who's ticked off that he's suddenly in my living room."

James laughed and crossed his heart. "I promise. One squirrel-free tree, ma'am." He looked at Oscar, who had dozed off again. "You don't think he'd try to climb it, would he?"

Amanda shook her head. "Takes too much effort, and he's too fat. I think the tree's safe."

He caught the nearly-wistful expression on Amanda's face. "What is it?"

She picked up the nearby broom, obviously uncomfortable. "Oh, nothing. I was just thinking that this Christmas is going to be so different than the ones I've had in the past. This year everything seems really..." she groped for the right word, "...traditional."

At his look of surprise, she explained. "I never had traditional. Not traditional *anything*. When Mom was alive we'd give each other a gift on Christmas Eve, and after she passed away, I'd go to my aunt and uncle's apartment for Christmas. We'd eat a big meal without anyone talking and then I'd sit and watch TV with them. I couldn't wait to get out the door." She shrugged, sweeping up the stray needles that littered the hardwood floor. "Not exactly Norman Rockwell."

Picking up the dustpan, James nodded. "That must've been rough. My family has a lot of traditions, maybe too many. If my Mom tries to make me eat one more slice of her fruitcake, I'm gonna lose it."

"Hey, I kinda like fruitcake."

"You're crazy, lady." James crouched down to hold the pan so she could sweep the needles toward him. "I know you're going to have the Christmas Eve party here at the Inn, but it sounds like it ends early enough that you could go with me to the candlelight late service at the Presbyterian church. Starts at nine. Both my nieces are going to be in the nativity pageant. You want to go with me?"

Amanda gripped the broom handle as James dumped the needles in a nearby trashcan. She'd met some of James' family, but not his two nieces. "Your whole family's going to be there?"

"Yep, the whole clan. If Derek can get there, I mean. He's on call for the fire station."

Amanda was still considering his invitation. She couldn't remember ever being to a Christmas service before. Most of the times she'd stepped into a church had been for weddings and funerals. The thought of being in a packed church, with James' family in the same pew, kind of made her nervous.

She tucked the broom in the hall closet, still thinking. "James, I didn't know you were a religious person."

Brushing his hands together, he flopped down on the nearest sofa. "I don't consider myself religious." He grinned at her. "I consider myself a man of faith. There's a difference."

Oscar had been watching and the moment he saw an open lap, he jumped down from his chair and up onto James, purring loudly as soon as James started scratching under his chin. Settling onto the tall man's chest, the big orange cat's eyes closed in contentment.

"I never grew up in a church, either, Amanda. One day a friend in high school had me read the gospel of John, and I was hooked. I'd thought church was all about following rules and it turns out I was wrong."

"No rules?" she settled into Oscar's abandoned chair, glad for the heat of the coffee she'd set on the table when James had arrived, and for the dying embers still in the fireplace. "Doesn't sound like any church I know. What about the whole 'thou shalt not steal', and all that sort of stuff? Aren't those rules?'"

"Well, if we were treating the other person the way we'd want to be treated, we wouldn't be stealing from him, would we? That whole 'love your neighbor' thing covers a lot." He waited, watching her as she sipped her coffee. "If you want to go with me, that'd be great."

"Let me guess. The girls are going to be dressed as angels for the pageant."

He smiled. "Actually, I think Hanna's gonna be a sheep."

"So if I go, no pressure?"

"I promise. No one's gonna make you eat a live chicken or try to convert you. I swear." He winked at her, still smiling, and she couldn't help but smile back.

"Maybe. I'll think about it."

Chapter 22

Winter in Oregon was a new experience for Amanda. A day could start with fog and move to rain, only to have a crystal-clear sky that night and sharp spikes of frost on the grass the next morning. Now that the rain had stopped even a cloudy sky made her happy, as long as she wasn't out getting wet in the weather.

Sometimes Amanda just liked to sit on one of the benches that surrounded the town square, and watch the people go by. The first few weeks after she'd moved to Ravenwood Cove she just watched, but now that she was part of the town most of the people passing her bench would wave and smile or stop and chat. At first, she missed the anonymity she'd had in LA, where people would walk by and pretend not to see you, but after a couple of months she'd become used to people looking her in the eye and wishing her a good morning when they walked past, or when she brushed by them in a store.

It was nice to be *seen*.

The town square was decked out in its best holiday finery. The same huge fir tree was decorated for Christmas every year. It was so tall that a local utility company let the town borrow one of its trucks with a crane-type basket, so that the lights would be checked and the gold star attached at the very top. Amanda had missed the tree-lighting ceremony due to helping some guests at the Inn, but even in the daytime, the town Christmas tree was a festive bit of beauty.

The Hortman brothers seemed to be doing a lot of business with their Christmas tree lot, playing holiday music to get people in the mood to buy a tree or a wreath, and just about every shop lining the square had decorated their windows and doors with lights. Even the town hall, normally a kind of formal brick building, looked more welcoming with loops of cedar garland and tiny fairy bulbs hanging from the front.

Turning her face toward the cold sun, Amanda closed her eyes and smiled. Even with the breeze making the sun's heat almost imperceptible, it felt so good to sit outside.

"Don't let that sunshine fool you. We're supposed to have some weather coming in the next couple of days, you know."

She cracked her eye open and smiled at Solomon Culpepper. "Morning, Solomon. What sort of weather?"

He gestured at the empty spot on the bench next to and she scooted over a bit, inviting him to sit down.

"Big windstorm. This is your first winter here, right? We get winter storms rolling through every once in a while but this one looks like it may be a doozy."

Amanda's thoughts instantly went to the Ravenwood Inn, and what she'd need to do to get it prepared for a big storm. "How big?"

"Well, if I were you I'd think about what to do if you lost power or if some of your trees get blown down. You know how the trees are sculpted on the cliffs over the Cove? The ones that look like they're leaning backwards?"

She did. The perpetually windblown trees looked like they'd had some bizarre trimming that made the ocean-facing branches shorter than the ones on the back. "Yes, I do. Some of my trees look a little like that, too."

"Well, even if they're old trees that have been through a lot of storms, you may still have a problem. Do you have a chainsaw?"

In all the time she'd been owner of the Ravenwood Inn, she'd never even considering having a chainsaw. "Um, no, I don't. Do I need to get one?"

Solomon shook his head. "Well, probably not. They're good to have in case of emergency but you can probably get someone to help you out, if you need one. Lots of people around here have tools that could help with a downed tree. Also, don't forget that the Ravenwood's not hooked up to city water. If you lose power, you lose water because your well will stop working."

"Thanks for the news, Solomon. I'll see what I can do to get ready."

Great. More things for the To Do list, she thought. *Maybe I'll go price generators.*

Solomon looked up at the clear sky. "Well, I'd better be going. Have to get my place all prepared and pick up some groceries. Talk to you later, Amanda," he said, and with a friendly wave, he was striding away from her down the sidewalk.

Amanda idly watched him walk away, still thinking about what she should do to get ready for the storm, when she saw Solomon pull something from his pocket.

It was a scarf.

A very distinctive, hand-knitted red and green scarf.

One that she'd seen before, at the train depot.

He wrapped it around his neck, and time seemed to stand still as her thoughts coalesced around the fact that Solomon was wearing something that she'd seen the same place the diamond necklace had been hidden.

Whether Desmond Martin had hidden Moonlight or Solomon had, she wasn't going to take any chances.

Making sure that Solomon was completely out of earshot, Amanda picked up her phone and dialed James' number, her fingers trembling.

Chapter 23

Amanda hadn't been at the arrest, but James had been all business when Amanda called to tell him how Solomon was wearing a scarf that she'd seen at the abandoned train depot. James' words had been short and clipped as he took down just the information he needed, and got off the phone to accost Solomon. By the time Amanda had gotten back to the Ravenwood Inn, Lisa had already left a message, saying she'd heard that the handyman had been put in the back seat of a cop car and been driven away.

Amanda listened to the voicemail but when she began to call Lisa back she hesitated a bit. She always wanted to talk to her friend, but this call sounded a bit like Lisa was wanting to see if Amanda knew anything about what had happened. Sometimes the lines between being Lisa being her friend and being the local reporter were a bit blurry, and Amanda had to be very careful about what she told her.

Finally deciding not to return Lisa's call, she headed upstairs to make a list of what she could to get ready for the upcoming windstorm. Her only guests had cancelled that morning, so her concern could be for the Inn itself, and not how to entertain people if there was no electricity.

It was a full day later before James swung by the Inn. The wind had already kicked up outside a bit, with blowing leaves and powerful gusts, and James had to push on the front door to shut it behind him when he came in.

"Looks like it about blew you off your feet." Amanda was curled up on the sofa with Oscar and a good book, enjoying the beauty of the huge Christmas tree. "How are you?"

He plopped down into the overstuffed chair on the other side of the fireplace, putting down a leather case and stretching his long legs out in front of him. "If I were a kite, I'd be in the next county by now. Whew!" He looked at her and smiled. "Figured you'd want to know the news."

"You bet I do."

"So, we picked Solomon up after your tip, and questioned him."

"Yes?" Book forgotten, she waited for what he had to say.

"Turns out that was the same scarf that was down at the Lucky Rail depot."

Amanda clapped her hands together. "I knew it!"

James ignored her enthusiasm. "And, it turns out that he had been at the depot before you were there, and after you were there. He confessed to being there, even though he's not saying much else, and his fingerprints were all over the cargo room. Only one problem."

"What's that?"

"No fingerprints of his in the stationmaster office. We knew that any prints there may have been compromised by your touching things in there, but we didn't find any of Solomon's. We did find several that belonged to Desmond Martin, and lots of partials and probably old fingerprints. Yours are undoubtedly in that room, too, so I brought you a present. Well, it's more like I'm going to let you use my toy." Opening the leather case, he pulled out an electronic device.

"IPad?" she quipped, knowing that she was wrong.

He shook his head. "Mobile fingerprint scanner. Let's see those lovely hands of your, Miss Graham. We need to rule out your prints."

She sighed but watched him input her information, and then showed her how to press her fingertips against the screen so it could map her prints. As soon as the machine had done its job, he picked up her hand and kissed the back of it, then released it with a grin.

"Thanks. This'll make the lab guys really happy."

She scooted Oscar out of her warm spot on the sofa, and sat back down. "Well, I'm all about making the lab guys happy. Did Solomon say what he was doing at the depot? He's not homeless, is he?"

James shook his head. "No, he's got a nice little cottage over by Mrs. Granger's place. He won't tell me what he was doing at the depot, not a word. Even though he's really shaken up by being arrested, he won't talk."

"Maybe he has some secrets of his own." She bit her bottom lip, considering what sort of secrets a handyman might have, and that he would sit in jail rather than disclose what he knew.

James was watching her, and she finally had an idea. "Can I go talk to him?"

Sitting up, James made a face. "Not a good idea. He's already been questioned and he's not cooperating at all. The best thing for him is to sit and stew a bit, and then tell us what we need to know."

"What if his secret isn't something he'd want to tell a man?"

James looked surprised. "What do you mean?"

"Well, all the officers at the station are male, right? What if he'd be a bit more talkative with a woman?"

"You mean you?" From the look on his face, Amanda knew James was intrigued. "Can't hurt, I guess. I'm heading back to the jail. Want a ride?"

Maybe it was strange to say that a ride in James' unmarked detective car was the most fun she'd had in a while but it was true. With Christmas music on the radio and them both telling embarrassing stories from their childhoods, their time driving through the windy town of Ravenwood Cove was full of laughter and teasing.

When they finally arrived at the jail, Amanda was surprised. She'd been expecting a more severe-looking building, but the brick exterior blended with the older structures in the area and didn't look institutional at all. James used his cardkey and buzzed them through the security door, waving at another officer and then stopping at the main desk. After a short conversation with the desk clerk and a signature on a clipboard, James escorted Amanda to a small room with several chairs and a square table. He gestured to a chair near the wall and then started to sit next to her, when Amanda put a hand on his arm.

"I think he'd talk more if you weren't here." When James started to protest, she put up a hand, her voice calm. "You can be right outside the door and see through the window. I'll be fine." She could see the conflicting thoughts on James' face, but he finally relented.

"I'll be right outside, and he'll know it."

She smiled, and James went out, leaving the door cracked open behind him.

Amanda could hear him speaking with someone outside, and then Solomon walked in the room, escorted by a police officer. With his orange jumpsuit and hands cuffed in front of him, he looked smaller and very different than his usual happy self. Once seated across from Amanda, the policeman turned to Amanda.

"You okay by yourself, Miss?"

Amanda smiled warmly at Solomon. "Yes, I am. I'm not worried."

Once the door clicked shut again, she turned to Solomon. He looked tired and a bit defensive, his lips a thin line as if he was intent on keeping them clenched shut.

"Who is she, Solomon?"

His eyes boggled in surprise. "What?"

"Who is she? The woman you've been meeting at the depot."

"I—"

Amanda leaned forward, pressing him a bit. "There's only one reason a man has a secret bed and a bottle of wine stashed, and that's because he doesn't want other people to know what he's doing romantically."

Solomon looked defiant, the first time Amanda had seen that look on his face. "I don't know what you're talking about."

Amanda smiled warmly. "Yes, you do. It must be lonely since Bertie left."

He turned away from her, refusing to answer.

"Solomon, if you don't tell these officers who you've been meeting down at the depot, they can't let you out of here."

His words were almost a whisper. "I don't want to hurt anyone."

Taking deep breath, Amanda nodded. "I know you don't. Do you want to call someone to see if it's okay with them to tell the truth? You can use my phone."

Solomon's eyes lit up, even though he hesitated. "I'd like that." Amanda handed him her phone and watched as he punched in a phone number. When it started to ring, she turned and studiously looked at the blank wall. It was the most privacy she could give him, because if she went out of the room the officers would want to know why.

A bit of muttered conversation, a couple of brief pauses, and then Solomon gave a deep, relieved sigh.

"Thank you, sweetheart. I'll see you soon." Amanda turned her head and Solomon handed the phone back to her.

Taking a shaky breath, he finally told the truth. "I've been seeing Sally Marino for almost a month now."

Amanda thought back through all the people she'd met locally and came up blank. "I'm not sure I know her."

Solomon nodded. "Yes, you do. She's the assistant manager at Petrie's."

The lightbulb clicked on in Amanda's head. "Oh! *That* Sally!" She remembered vaguely that Mrs. Granger had once told her that Sally was married but that her husband was in a local nursing home, suffering from the last stages of Alzheimer's. "She seems very sweet."

Solomon seemed to relax as soon as he heard Amanda's comment. "She is very sweet, and she's a really good person. We just didn't want anyone to know about us because her husband is sick and my wife is gone." He leaned forward, his face earnest. "You wouldn't believe the amount of gossip that happens in Ravenwood Cove."

"So I've heard." She thought back to some of the chitchat she'd heard in the past. She'd have to be more careful to not be part of that.

"I didn't want people to think bad things about Sally. She's got a good heart and she's basically been by herself for over four years now. That's a long time for someone young to be alone."

Amanda nodded in sympathy. "I'll bet it is. Solomon, did you know anything about the Moonlight Necklace?"

"I don't know anything about that danged necklace and I wish people would stop asking me about it! If I'd known it was there, I would've turned it in for the reward and gotten myself a divorce. Or maybe fixed up my place."

Amanda nodded. "Do I have your permission to tell the officers what you were doing at the depot? I think it will make a big difference on how soon you get out of here."

There was a pause while Solomon considered his options. "If you just tell James Landon, I'm okay with it," he finally said. "I think he could keep a secret."

They smiled at each other, both relieved, and Amanda got up to open the door.

"I'll let him know he can come in now."

Chapter 24

When Amanda stopped by Cuppa in the late afternoon for a mocha, she found her usually chipper friend, Meg, was all a flutter. She was almost running back and forth across the coffeeshop, tucking away outside decorations and turning off the lights in the pastry case.

When she saw it was Amanda coming through the door, she looked relieved. "Go turn over the CLOSED sign, would ya?" she asked as she picked up a broom. "Can you believe this wind? Taking the trash out and locking the dumpster was like getting punched by a cold fist."

Flipping the sign, Amanda watched Meg with alarm. "Are you okay? I thought you were going to be open for another twenty minutes or so."

Meg shook her head and picked up a broom. "Not on a day like this. I've been watching the weather channel all morning and it looks like we're going to get the full brunt of the storm. I'm closing up shop early and heading home to build a fire in the fireplace and eat Christmas cookies." She shuddered. "I hate storms."

It didn't take long for Meg to rope Amanda into helping her put away everything and clean the coffeeshop for the night. As she wiped down the long display case, Amanda started thinking about all the people around Ravenwood Cove that could be affected by a storm like this. There were a lot of folks who made their living outdoors, whether it was on the sea fishing or in the woods with the lumber industry. She wondered how much this would impact them. She'd seen the wild waves and fierce wind of coastal storms when she lived in California, but this was the first time she'd seen them farther north.

Meg was wiping down the tables, when a thought suddenly occurred to her. "Amanda, did I tell you that Truman's started wearing a kilt sometimes? One of those macho, modern ones?"

Amanda burst out in laughter. "Figures. That's exactly the sort of thing he'd do." She tried to picture her friend in a kilt. Not a pretty picture. "Well, then there's just one good thing about this winter windstorm."

"What's that?" Meg asked.

Amanda grinned at her. "At least it makes Truman put on a pair of pants."

By the time they'd gotten everything cleaned and put away the power was starting to flicker, then dull to a brownish hue. Just as they stepped out into the swirling coldness, there was a brilliant flash that lit up the sky, and the electricity died as the town plunged in murky, late-afternoon darkness.

"Transformer blew," Meg explained, as if expecting it. She had to nearly shout to be heard above the whining wind. "It'll be awhile before they get that fixed. We'll be lucky if we keep cell service. We're supposed to be getting lightning and thunder later. You okay at the Inn tonight, or do you want to come to my place?"

Amanda shook her head. "I'm going home. Jennifer said she wanted to do some cleaning and I'll bet Oscar is hiding under one of the beds. Besides," she said with a smile, "the safest place around is probably the oldest building that's been through all this stuff before." She hugged Meg tightly and they both walked to their cars, their hands stuffed in their pockets and their heads tucked down against the battering wind.

***

On the drive home, Amanda had to wrestle the steering wheel for control of the car. She could feel the relentless storm pushing against her SUV and shaking it as she drove carefully back to the Inn. Puffs of freezing air were pushing through the gaskets around her door and window, and she turned up the heater as far as it could go. A couple of times she had to dodge falling tree limbs as the violently-shaken trees had branches ripped from them. Pulling into her driveway, she tried to open the front door but it was locked tight. Jennifer must've gone home already. Sliding her key into the lock, she practically blew into the foyer, the wind pushing her inside as she slammed the door against it.

Oscar was sitting unrepentantly on the Inn's marble kitchen island, apparently unconcerned about the sound of the storm shaking the old Inn. When Amanda walked into the kitchen and called to him, he jumped down and sat beside his food dish. Amanda had missed his feeding time and he was going to make sure she knew it.

"Glad to see someone has their priorities straight around here," she told him, using her cell phone as a temporary flashlight while she headed to the pantry for his food.

The old Inn creaked and groaned as the howling winds battered it, but stood fast. It was already dark outside, so Amanda couldn't see much, but she could occasionally hear thumps on the siding and roof as debris or branches hit the building. She lit some of her lanterns and set them around the front parlor, enjoying their soft glow. The one on the small table by the sofa gave plenty of light for reading, and she tried to lose herself in a book while the storm raged on outside.

As much as she tried to concentrate on the words, though, she just couldn't. Her mind kept drifting back to her talk with Solomon and his telling her about Sally. With him definitely not a suspect anymore, it meant that whoever killed Desmond Martin hadn't been caught yet.

She finally gave up attempting to read and lay down on the couch, pulling the heavy quilt up to her neck against the chill in the room. Trying to doze and ignore the sounds of the storm outside, she shut her eyes and relaxed, thinking about her day.

As her mind drifted, separate little pieces of conversation and what she'd observed started to come together. Details of everything that had happened began to coalesce as she turned them over in her mind, slowly crystallizing until one single, horrible, thought formed.

She sat up with a gasp, suddenly fully awake.

She knew who'd killed Desmond Martin.

Chapter 25

"Let me in, Mrs. Welch. It's Amanda Graham. I need to talk to you!"

Amanda could see the lady moving behind the translucent curtains by the front door.

"I know you're in there!" Even with the wind howling around her she was sure her voice would carry.

There was a click and the door was reluctantly cracked open. Not seeing a chain across the top, Amanda pushed against the door and shoved Mrs. Welch into the dark foyer.

"What are you doing? Get out!" Mrs. Welch hollered.

Amanda gasped as Mrs. Welch smacked her. Grabbing the confused lady's arm, she nearly shouted, "I know who killed Desmond Martin, and you're in grave danger."

Mrs. Welch's mouth formed a silent O. "I...I don't know what you're talking about. I had nothing to do with his death!"

"No, but your necklace did." Amanda gripped Mrs. Welch's upper arms, knowing she was scaring her. We need to get out of here. Have you seen anyone nearby, maybe around the house?"

As soon as Amanda had figured out who the killer was, she also realized that the storm would be a perfect cover for them to come back for a second try to steal

Moonlight. No electricity, no phone calls. It was a perfect and deadly opportunity.

"No, nobody. The house is locked up tight."

Amanda felt a surge of relief, but as she tried to get Mrs. Welch to walk toward the door, the older lady balked.

"I'm not leaving without Moonlight! I can't!"

Amanda gripped her arm, nearly desperate. "We need to leave now. I think you've got a killer after you who still wants that necklace."

For the first time, Amanda saw a flash of resolve cross Mrs. Welch's thin face. "It's the last thing I have of my husband's and I'm taking it with me. You can leave if you want, but I'm going to go get Moonlight before I go.

"Where's the necklace now?"

"It's...um..it's in the safe. I can get it in sixty seconds."

"Go get it, and hurry."

Mrs. Welch grabbed her flashlight and headed up the stairs, Amanda trailing behind. The pool of light in front of them was so narrow Amanda made sure to keep one hand on the older lady's back as they ascended.

James. She needed to try to reach James.

"Do you have a landline? I can't get my cellphone to work."

Mrs. Welch gripped the top of the stair railing and turned, surprised. Amanda could barely see her face in the dark. "No, I gave it up months ago, when it got too expensive."

Amanda followed her into a small parlor next to the stairs. From what she could see, it was nearly empty of furniture, with only a heavy wooden table and an old sofa. Any carpets or antiques were long gone, and their footsteps creaked across the bare wood floor.

A sudden flash of daylight-bright lightning lit up the room, making Mrs. Welch give a sudden yelp. A deafening boom of thunder rolled right over it. The storm was nearly on top of them.

"It's in here," Mrs. Welch said, walking to the fireplace and handing the flashlight to Amanda. She fiddled with a bit of tile near the mantel and it finally swung open, revealing the circular dial of a hidden wall safe.

Amanda felt her heart racing as Mrs. Welch turned the dial slowly clockwise. If she could just get both of them to safety they could ride out the storm, or find someone who could call out to the authorities.

There was a creak on the floorboards in the hallway. A single creak.

Amanda lunged for Mrs. Welch and practically pulled her to the floor, the flashlight flying from her hand as dove for the space behind the sofa. It spun wildly on the wood, finally pointing toward a dark corner of the room. The thin beam of light barely illuminated the rest of the room.

Amanda had landed almost on top of Mrs. Welch, who was gasping in surprise and doing her best to push Amanda off her. Quickly shushing her, Amanda froze, straining her ears to listen for any tiny sounds that would tell her if her horrible suspicions were true.

There was no sound, but Amanda could nearly feel the malevolent presence that stood in the hallway.

"I know it's you, Celia."

There was a pause, then the sound of a gun being cocked.

"So what." The voice was flat and emotionless, and very familiar.

Mrs. Welch's eyes were round with terror. Amanda looked at her, gathering her courage, and went on.

"I know you killed Desmond Martin."

A faint sound of a sigh. "How did you know?"

"You knew about Desmond Martin's criminal past, but that was never in the newspaper, was it? Nobody in town knew he had a record, except for you."

Silence.

Amanda continued. "If you knew about his past, that means you knew him when he was at the bakery that day, supposedly applying for a job." She tried to keep her voice steady, even though her heart was beating a mile a minute.

"Open the safe." The words were nearly hissed.

Amanda's mind was racing, trying to think how to outsmart the armed killer who would do anything for Moonlight. Maybe she could make Celia crack, to drop her guard enough that they could escape.

"He hadn't grabbed you to harass you. He was your boyfriend. You just got caught with him that day in the bakery and so you *said* he'd grabbed you." Amanda waited, straining to hear any response.

Silence.

Amanda kept on, looking around to see if there was anything she could use as a weapon. "Nice acting with those tears, though. You fooled me. Sure sounds like you fooled poor Mrs. Mason, too. "

There was a pause. "That's not my fault."

"Nice way to treat someone you said was like your mother."

The venom in the disembodied voice was real. "You don't know anything about my mother."

"I know that Desmond Martin had a new Jayhawk tattoo on his leg. I saw it when I found his body and had to see if he was dead. If he's from around here, why would he have a tattoo of a Kansas Jayhawk? Was it because he thought he was important enough to someone that he should honor her by putting that picture on his skin?"

The voice, bitter, floated on the dead air.

"I never asked him to get that stupid tattoo."

Amanda took a deep breath, realizing she was playing a very dangerous game. "No, but you knew that he loved you, didn't you? You knew that he'd do anything for you, even steal the diamond necklace you wanted so desperately. What did you say to him to get him to do that, Celia? Why did he want to steal Moonlight for you?"

"Mine." The word was soft, and the voice had moved.

Amanda silently eased off Mrs. Welch, pushing her farther behind the sofa.

Amanda took a deep breath. "Celia Welch. That's your real name. You're Mr. Welch's daughter, aren't you?"

"Moonlight's mine. Mama told me it was always meant to be mine." There was a note of pain in Celia's words.

Mrs. Welch's eyes were wide with shock.

Amanda could see a heavy-looking vase on the edge of the mantelpiece, maybe made out of metal. She had to keep Celia talking.

"What happened to you, Celia? What did your father do to you?"

There was a sharp bark of laughter. "You mean, where did he throw me away? Me and my mother? Can't you guess where he dumped us like garbage and left us so he could make a new life with a new wife?"

Kansas.

Mrs. Welch's voice was trembling, but brave. "If you hurt either one of us, we won't open the safe for you, but if you let us go you can have the necklace. I don't want it, really. It's yours. Just let us walk out of here and you can go wherever you like."

They waited.

"I can't let you go." There was a shifting sound, as if Celia was leaning against the wall. "I just want this to be over."

Mrs. Welch took a deep breath. "Honey, I never even knew you existed, I swear. I'd heard the rumors but when I talked to your father he denied everything. He swore to me that he'd never been married before. I would've been happy to have you be part of our lives."

A quick sob, then the voice was hard again.

"Figures he didn't tell you about me. Bastard."

Amanda patted Mrs. Welch's leg to get her attention, moving her hand as if it was talking.

Keep her talking, she motioned, and Mrs. Welch nodded.

"I'm so sorry, honey," she tried, as Amanda silently eased upward, still behind the sofa. The heavy vase was nearly three feet past the safety of cover, but they had no other weapon except their voices and their wit. She peeked carefully over the edge of the couch, trying to see if Celia was standing there.

A brilliant flash of lightning flared, illuminating the room as if it were daylight. Amanda held her breath, watching, and waiting for the thunder.

She could see Celia peering around the doorjamb, her eyes wild and ringed with white.

Darkness fell again. Booming thunder shook the house as Amanda leaped toward the fireplace, desperately grabbing for the metal vase. It was heavier than she'd thought it would be, and just as she turned she could hear Celia pivoting into the parlor, suddenly aware that Amanda had come out from behind the sofa.

The gun was held in front of her, shaking but trained directly at Amanda.

"Give me Moonlight!" Celia yelled as she strode toward Amanda, who was still holding the awkward vase.

Mustering every bit of strength she had, Amanda ducked to the side and hurled the heavy container at Celia's head.

There was a flash of light and a sharp crack of a gunshot as Amanda dove out of the bullet's path. The vase smashed into the side of Celia's temple, rocking her head sideways with the force. Her knees crumpled beneath her, the pistol flying from her hand as she careened backward. The vase seemed to explode as it hit the hard floor, spewing a sudden cloud of dust and ash everywhere as the top flew off.

Amanda sprang to her feet and grabbed the pistol with both hands, standing over the nearly-unconscious Celia.

Mrs. Welch came out from behind the sofa and grabbed the flashlight. "That was my husband's ashes," she said flatly, training the beam of light on the bits of grit and powder all over the floor.

Amanda didn't feel any sympathy. "Mrs. Welch! Run to the neighbors and see if anyone has a phone that works. Get the cops!" She could feel the adrenaline coursing through her as she watched Celia for any movement.

Mrs. Welch nodded her head at Amanda's words and gave her the flashlight, then pelted down the stairs as if her life depended on it. Amanda could hear the front door being flung open, then slamming behind Mrs. Welch as she ran from the house.

Chapter 26

Ivy's Café was packed with people, the cold workers hungry after a long morning cleaning up the storm damage from two days before. Every booth and table was filled with townspeople peeling off their jackets and gloves, laughing and greeting each other as they sat down to order. Someone had been plugging the jukebox with quarters, and apparently had a taste for Elvis and Chuck Berry. Ruby opened up the back room, normally used for meetings, and within minutes every seat in the place was full.

"Hey, everybody!" Ruby shouted, trying to get the crowd's attention. After a few seconds the conversations died down, with just the jukebox playing.

"We've got plenty of food and are thrilled you are all here, but it's gonna take some time for us to serve all of you. Does anyone want to help out waitressing so we can get the food out to everyone as fast as possible?"

Within minutes she had two volunteers, including Jennifer Peetman, and Grace TwoHorses had said she'd be happy to help in the kitchen. Ruby grinned and thanked everyone, a relieved smile on her face as she hustled from table to table, taking orders.

Amanda was crammed in the back of a padded booth, Lisa on one side and James holding her hand on the other. Meg and Mrs. Granger sat opposite her, and it seemed like everyone in town strolled by to chat and congratulate her on catching Desmond Martin's killer. While she'd been working with everyone to pick up the storm debris and assess the damage, she couldn't count how many times she'd been hugged or had someone say that they were so glad she was okay.

Amanda watched the crowd around her with a sense of wonder. She could see Solomon and Truman at a nearby table, discussing jazz music, and George Ortiz had brought his entire family to be part of the cleanup crew. Madeline Wu and Mrs. Mason were obviously plotting something, as they had their heads together and were talking intensely, probably about their latest business ideas. For once, Henry Crabbe had showed up in town without his metal detector, and had gamely been shoved into a booth with the Hendersons, who were questioning him about how to find rare coins. Mrs. Sandford was at a table for two, carefully wiping down the tabletop with a napkin and trying to ignore the fact that Brian Petrie was sitting opposite her.

Amanda looked at the crowd with relief and gratitude. It was amazing to be here in this crowded café, waiting for food that would take ages to get to her, and sitting with dear friends. She was happy to be alive.

"So, how's Celia doing these days, being in jail and all?" Mrs. Granger asked James, while trying to look innocent and failing entirely.

"Fine. Are you asking me if the quotes in the paper about her not being sorry are true or not?"

Lisa sat up straight. "Hey, those quotes are correct! She was yelling all the time she was being put in back of the cop car, even after she'd been read her rights. She said she didn't think she'd done anything wrong."

Mrs. Granger just smiled, waiting, and James finally smiled back. "The quotes were correct."

Meg's mouth dropped open. "How could she not think she'd done anything wrong? She killed one guy in cold blood so she could keep the necklace, then tried to kill two more to get it later?" She shook her head. "I don't understand some people. Why would Desmond Martin steal the necklace for her, then hide the key so she couldn't get it?"

"I'll bet I know. Let me see what James thinks of this theory," Amanda said, turning toward the detective. "My guess is that he thought he'd sell the necklace and they'd use the money for a life together, but Martin had doubts about whether Celia really wanted to be with him or if she just wanted Moonlight for herself. Is that about right?"

James nodded. "She thought he had the key on him when he died, but she couldn't find it, so she had to wait until someone found the necklace before she could try to get it for herself again." He smiled at Amanda. "You should've been a detective. Oh wait, you almost *are* a detective in this town, aren't you?"

Amanda laughed. "Not hardly. My sleuthing days are over." She took a deep breath. "You know, when I moved to this little town I was worried that nothing was ever going to happen around here."

Mrs. Granger pushed aside her huge slice of carrot cake and poured herself more coffee, ignoring her granddaughter's quiet attempt at stopping her. "Then you don't know Ravenwood Cove," she said. "This place is full of weirdos and secrets. I'm the head weirdo."

They laughed, but Amanda still had questions. "So, how did Celia find out her father was in Ravenwood?"

"Obituary," James said. "Mrs. Welch put his death notice in the Ravenwood Tide, and it gets put on the internet. Celia came looking for what she thought was her inheritance, the necklace. She couldn't find or open the safe, so she just waited until she found someone who could. Then after she met Desmond and found out that he'd probably be able to open the safe, she started a relationship with him so that he'd steal Moonlight for her. When he told her he wanted a new life with her and that he wanted to sell the necklace, she killed him. Guess she thought that he had the necklace on him or she'd be able to find it in his things, but she couldn't."

"It's really sad," Amanda added. "Mrs. Welch told me she never knew anything about his other family, and that she'd never seen him do anything but be a loving husband. She only found out about the money issues and get-rich-quick schemes when he died and she went through all his things, including his computer. Once the debtors read the obituary and found where he was they came knocking, and she had to sell almost everything she owned to just pay them off. Apparently, she'd been secretly sending her furniture and jewelry to Mrs. Sanford's gallery for the past several months, just trying to sell enough to keep afloat."

"Well, she won't have to worry about money now," Lisa said. "I heard she'd going to sell Moonlight at an auction in Portland, and that the estimate of its value is really high. She'll be able to have some peace and quiet in her big house, and be left alone."

Mrs. Granger, always opinionated, piped up. "I think that's a terrible idea. Not about selling the necklace. God knows it's brought nothing but trouble to that poor lady. I think it's a terrible idea for her to hide in that big house, no matter how much money she has. You know what she needs?" The old lady looked around the table, expectant. "She needs a job, and to get out around people. With Celia gone, Mrs. Mason is going to need someone to help out at the bakery, and I'll bet Mrs. Welch would be great at that." She carefully stood and grabbed the handles of her walker. If you'll excuse me, I think I'll go have a chat with Mrs. Mason and see what she thinks of my brilliant idea." Without a backward glance, the ninety-year-old do-gooder pushed her walker through the crowd, intent on getting her way.

They watched her go with admiration, and Meg spoke for them all. "Don't you just love the way she actually helps people, instead of just talking about it?"

James sighed. "Yes, I do."

Watching the waitresses zip by with plates of food, Lisa asked, "Hey, did anyone else see the forecast? We're supposed to be getting snow in the next day or so, maybe in time for Christmas."

Meg shook her head. "You know how rare snow is at sea level. I'd be surprised if we get a single flake. It'll get dumped all over the Coast Range, not here."

Lisa made a face. "Pessimist."

Amanda watched the faces of her friends and neighbors, and felt safe and happy. "I'm so sorry that the storm made the town cancel Hometown Holidays," she said sadly. "I was really looking forward to a Christmas festival."

James looked a bit surprised. "We couldn't have the festival with all the storm damage. There are still trees down across several of the roads, and the town's a mess. Besides," he added, "isn't it more fun with just the town all together? No tourists, no carnival?"

Ruby walked up to the table, carefully balanced platters of food on both arms, to a general cheer from the diners. Passing out the warm plates, she pulled a ketchup bottle from her apron pocket and hurried back to the kitchen for another pickup.

Mrs. Granger was coming back, pushing her walker and flashing a triumphant smile. "I talked to her," she announced as she pivoted her walker and sat down on the plastic seat. "Mrs. Mason said she'd be happy to talk to Mrs. Welch about giving her a trial run at the bakery."

"Amanda was just telling us she was sorry we had to cancel Hometown Holidays," Meg said, keeping her grandmother updated.

Mrs. Granger blew a raspberry. "Who needs a carnival when you've had so much excitement lately at Ravenwood Cove? How could a festival compete with what we've all been through recently?" She smiled at Amanda, her eyes kind, and Amanda found herself smiling back.

Indeed. It turned out she didn't need a carnival after all.

Epilogue

Christmas Eve in Ravenwood Cove was a wonder. After all the trouble of the storm and the cleanup, as well as catching the murderer, Celia Welch, having the merriness of Christmas was a welcome relief.

Ravenwood Inn had been known for decades as the place that the town came for an open house and Christmas Eve potluck, and Amanda had done her best to try to uphold that tradition. She'd hired Henry Crabbe as temporary help, and Jennifer Peetman had made sure to keep an eye on him as the historic bed and breakfast was scrubbed and polished. Amanda had struggled with the idea of how to set out all the food people were going to bring, until she remembered that hostesses of past parties must've known what they were doing, and set it up exactly as it had been decades ago. She'd even made Henry put extra strings of small white lights in the front trees, so that when the guests started to arrive, they gasped in wonder.

The old Inn was full of laughter and music, with the warm smells of dozens of homemade dishes threaded through everything. Oscar seemed to be in his element, perched on a comfy armchair by the fireplace and regally accepting attention from anyone who wanted to pet him. The huge Christmas tree was a huge hit, with anxious parents shooing kids away when they wanted to sample the candy canes hanging on branches. Even with the below-freezing cold, guests sometimes wandered out to the front porch, loving the soft glow of hanging lanterns and Christmas lights.

Just like in past years, the party wrapped up at nine o'clock sharp, with parents taking their children home to tuck into bed before Santa came, and other families getting ready to attend late evening church services.

Amanda was a bit nervous when she pulled on her heavy coat. She'd finally made the decision to sit with James and his family at the candlelight service, but it was definitely out of her comfort zone. James had been a wonderful help during the party, making sure that everyone was included and having a good time, while filling people's glasses and cracking jokes. She'd watched him easily move from conversation to conversation, always ready to make someone smile or pick up a discarded plate.

He was waiting downstairs, this tall detective, and she couldn't hide the fact that seeing a movie with him on a casual date was very different than being included in his family's holiday traditions. The thought of sitting in the same pew as his siblings and parents made her stomach hurt.

Looking in the bathroom mirror, Amanda gave a last touch-up to her lipstick and headed downstairs, trying to be brave.

The service was different than she expected. The church was packed, full of people dressed in their holiday best, or whatever would keep them warm. There was lots of music, including a children's choir, and different people reading the Christmas story. Pastor Fox gave a talk about the true meaning of Christmas and said that Christmas was about God showing us that we weren't just some lab experiment that had been created and then left to fend for itself. He added that God had proven his continuing love by giving the greatest sacrifice he could show humans that they would understand. Amanda had always liked Pastor Fox but she'd been halfway expecting some judgmental speech, so it was a bit of a surprise.

Amanda was also surprised how many of the old Christmas carols she remembered, singing along a bit timidly and trying not to laugh at James' booming baritone as he belted them out with gusto. His family had been warm and friendly, without asking too many questions or making her uncomfortable, but they obviously thought of her as James' girlfriend, which was a first.

Looking around the church, Amanda could see dozens of people she knew. Mrs. Granger was back a couple of rows, and had gleefully waved a brand-new cellphone at Amanda when she'd seen her. Apparently, Meg had given her grandmother exactly what she'd wanted for Christmas.

Toward the end of the service, ushers passed out white candles with cardboard rings that slipped on, to protect people from getting splashed by hot wax. The lights were slowly dimmed, then turned off, and Pastor Fox talked about the importance of the light moving into the darkness. He took his lit candle and touched it to the candle belonging to the person next to him, then to another person, as the slow flicker of faint light began to grow around her, Amanda could see many happy faces reflecting the golden flames. As the candles were slowly lit around the church, Pastor Fox watched until he was sure every person there had a candle, and then began to sing Silent Night.

This was music that Amanda hadn't experienced before, with no instruments or recordings or conductors. It was a groundswell of rich sound, sung with emotion and years of Christmas memories. The purity of it caught her off guard, and she sang along, loving being part of its beauty. At the end of the hymn, voices trailed off, as if wanting to continue, and there was a profound stillness. After a minute or so, a few lights were turned back on, and people shuffled toward the back of the church, blowing out their candles and putting them in a box by the door.

Holding James' hand, Amanda made her way through the crowd, following his family to the double doors. As they opened, there was a collective sigh from the churchgoers. Amanda moved her head around to get her a better look as the congregation started walking down the front steps.

Stepping out of the church's front doors was like walking into a hushed snow globe. The town square was silent, every noise muffled by the soft, white snow covering the town square, already a couple of inches deep over the grass. Fat snowflakes were continuing to fall, icing the small town of Ravenwood Cove in a winter glaze. The town's permanent Christmas tree, with its lights repaired as much as possible after the recent storm, stood tall and proud, red ribbons on its branches waving in the breeze.

"If I'd known if would be like this, I would've brought one of the sleighs from the ranch." James was smiling. "The draft horses would love it."

Amanda sighed blissfully. "That would've been great. You know, I think this is my first white Christmas ever." At James' surprised expression, she explained. "You don't get this sort of thing in LA, you know."

James smiled. "There's more to Ravenwood Cove than just murder and mysteries, Miss Graham. You still have a lot left to discover around here."

Yes, I do, Amanda thought, and smiled back at James. Whatever the future may bring, she was truly looking forward to unraveling more secrets about Ravenwood Cove.

AUTHOR NOTES:

I really enjoyed getting to meet these characters again, and letting some of the more quiet ones into the forefront!

If you liked what you read, please consider leaving a review. Being an independent author means this is my own small business, and I appreciate any feedback you can give, so other readers will know if my writing is their cup of tea or not ☺ Thank you for stopping by!

Want to know about new releases, sale pricing, and exclusive content? Visit my website at http://CarolynDeanBooks.com/ and my email newsletter is HERE. Spam-free, and only sent out when there's something new, on sale, or FREE. I PROMISE.

THE ENTIRE RAVENWOOD COVE SERIES:

Book 1 - BED, BREAKFAST, and BONES

Book 2 - DUNE, DOCK, and a DEAD MAN

Book 3 - MISTLETOE, MOONLIGHT, and MURDER

Book 4 - SEA, SKY, and SKELETON

Book 5 - TIME, TIDE and TROUBLE

Book 6 - SUN, SAND, and SECRETS

RUTH'S CASHEW CHRISTMAS COOKIES

- ½ cup butter
- 1 cup brown sugar, firmly packed
- 1 egg
- ½ teaspoon real vanilla
- 1/3 cup dairy sour cream
- ¾ teaspoon baking powder
- ¾ teaspoon baking soda
- ¼ teaspoon salt
- 2 cups sifted flour
- 1 – ¾ cups whole or halves cashew nuts, salted

Preheat oven to 400 degree Fahrenheit.

Cream butter and sugar until light and fluffy.

Beat in egg and vanilla.

Add sifted dry ingredients alternately with sour cream.

Carefully fold in nuts. Drops by teaspoonful onto greased cookie sheet.

Bake 10 minutes at 400 degrees.

Cool and frost with butter frosting.

Top each cookie with a cashew nut.

Golden Butter Frosting:

- ½ cup butter
- 3 Tablespoons liquid coffee creamer or evaporated milk
- ¼ teaspoons real vanilla
- 2 cups sifted confectioners (powdered) sugar